THE M
TREE
MURDERS

An enthralling crime mystery full of twists

ROGER SILVERWOOD

Yorkshire Murder Mysteries Book 22

JOFFE BOOKS

Revised edition 2020
Joffe Books, London
www.joffebooks.com

First published in Great Britain in 2014

ISBN: 978-1-78931-654-4

ONE

Bromersley, South Yorkshire
Summer 2010

Helen was forty years of age. Her first marriage had been a disaster.

Single again at thirty-eight, she had assumed that the best men on the market would have already been snapped up and that she was going to have to settle for what was available — which, on looking around, didn't seem to be very much. She had thought she may even have to live with a man on a trial basis, which she was not entirely averse to. She hoped her judgement a second time might be less driven by sex and more concerned with long-time love and trust, and the possibility of becoming a mother, even at her age. She had always wanted children but her ex had not shown any desire to be a father. In fact, he had always insisted on her taking the pill, which had been a bone of contention between them.

After moving back in with her loving but straight-laced elderly parents for two years, which wasn't easy after running her own household, she had left and rented a flat. Shortly afterwards, her father died. It was naturally distressing for mother and daughter, and Helen considered the inevitability of having to return to the family house.

Then she had met Paul Rose. He was a kind man. He had also been married before; his wife had left him unexpectedly. Paul was backward at coming forward but they formed a gentle relationship that quietly flourished until each understood the other and they slowly fell in love. He was a handsome man of thirty-nine, who worked at a local garage, servicing cars. They had a holiday together which bonded them even more. Then, unexpectedly, her mother died. Helen was on the floor again, but Paul Rose lifted her up.

Helen inherited quite an estate from her mother, so they wasted no more time. They seemed to be right for each other. On 10 August 2013, they married quietly in St Mary's Church, Bromersley.

In November, an old stone house on Creesforth Road called The Brambles came on to the market at a very reasonable price. It had been the home of an elderly widower, Hubert Grant, who had owned an antiques and second-hand shop in Bromersley called Aladdin's Cave. He had died recently and his estate was being wound up by a local solicitor on behalf of the man's family.

One of the advantages of the old house was that included in the sale were some old pieces of furniture including all the entrance hall furniture and fittings and a wardrobe and a large bed in the master bedroom. The house was rather big for Paul and Helen Rose, but as they both lived in hope of having children, they snapped it up and moved in. They engaged a 'daily', Cora Blenkinsop, a pleasant, willing, talkative young woman, to come for a few hours a day to clean the place as it had been neglected during the latter period of the previous owner's lifetime.

One day, as Cora was scrubbing the terracotta tiles on the kitchen floor, she said, 'Of course, Mrs Rose, much as I like you and Mr Rose and I love working for you here, and I wouldn't mind working evenings here now and again, if ever you wanted me to, I wouldn't like to live here permanently. I mean, I wouldn't want to spend the *night* here.'

Helen Rose blinked, turned away from the cupboard where she was reaching for the salt to season the soup she was making, and said, 'Oh? Why?'

'Well, you must have heard the stories . . . ?'

'No. No. I haven't heard anything, Cora.'

'Well, the appearances . . . the er . . . *apparitions*, I think they call them.'

Helen Rose smiled. 'No. I've not seen anything. What of?'

Cora Blenkinsop shuddered. 'Oh. The whole family of them has been seen . . . at different times . . . usually in the bedroom. Mrs Cudlipp comes in a long white dress. She was the wife of Amos Cudlipp. Now, he was a bad lot. He was a big man who wore a big top hat. He was a dentist *and* cattle slaughterer. They don't really go together. do they? Apparently he liked the bottle, was an alcoholic. And they had two children, a boy and a girl. Then there was another young girl, about fourteen, she was supposed to be a servant, a housemaid. Now Amos Cudlipp married when he was forty but his wife, poor soul, was only seventeen. They had two children pretty quickly, one after the other. Then his wife ran off, but Amos found her, dragged her back and kept her under lock and key for some time in that little bedroom at the back with the tiny window. They say it didn't have a window then. It's had one put in since but it's only very small.'

Helen Rose nodded. She had noticed that it was not like the other windows when she and her husband had looked round the house.

'Anyway,' Cora said, 'Amos's attentions then turned to the housemaid. He soon got her up the duff. When she gave him the news, something inside his head must have snapped. He got very drunk, got one of the knives he used for slaughtering cattle and murdered his wife, the two kids and the housemaid. After that he disappeared. A week later his body was found floating in the River Don . . . it was thought that he had drunk himself stupid and then drowned himself. The church wouldn't bury him in sacred ground. His body is here somewhere . . . in a grave . . . in the garden.'

Helen Rose's eyes narrowed. 'In the garden?'

It was unsettling to hear that Amos Cudlipp's body was anywhere near the house; it disturbed her more than she was prepared to admit but she wasn't going to let Cora see that the story had made any impression on her.

'Whereabouts in the garden?' she said.

'Eee, I don't know, Mrs Rose. There's supposed to be a cross over it.'

'What sort of a cross?'

'I don't know. I've never looked for it.'

'Where are the family and the housemaid buried then?'

'Oh, in the churchyard of St Mary's, I think. And that's all I know about it, Mrs Rose. It makes me go cold thinking about it. Look, I've got gooseflesh all up my arm.'

Helen Rose looked down at her. 'It's probably just a story, Cora. Don't think about it,' she said.

'Oh, they say it's *true*,' Cora said. 'I can't help but think about it, when I'm here, sometimes.'

Cora left at four o'clock and as the front door closed her provocative chattering was replaced with an echoing silence. All that could be heard was the hall clock ticking, and Helen Rose couldn't stop thinking about it either. When she tried to dismiss it, she couldn't. It dominated her thoughts; she was unnerved when she realized that she would be alone in the house for another hour and a half until Paul returned from the garage. She couldn't wait to tell him the story about Amos Cudlipp.

In the meantime, as she stirred the soup, and her pulse could be heard drumming in her ears, she silently listened out for any sound that indicated that she was not alone.

Zenith Television & Film Studios, Leeds, Yorkshire
Sunday, 10 November 2013, 9.30 p.m.

A thirty-year-old man in an immaculately pressed suit stood in front of the bank of cameras and teleprompters. He flashed a sparklingly white smile at the studio audience.

'Well, friends, as we come to the end of this exciting contest, here are the scores. I have managed to give away one hundred pounds to Marie from Chesterfield . . .'

There was applause from the studio audience.

'Thirteen thousand pounds to Joss from Dartmouth . . .'

More applause from the audience.

'But tonight's outstanding winner of *Wanna Be Rich?*, taking home sixty-two thousand pounds, is Josephine Huxley from Birmingham. Give her a big hand.'

There was even more deafening applause, whistles and stamping of feet.

'Will you come back next week, Josephine?'

She looked down and smiled nervously. 'Yes,' she said in a small voice.

'What a great sport you are, Josephine,' he said to her, then turned to the audience. 'Isn't she, ladies and gentlemen?' He clapped enthusiastically. 'And we'll look forward to seeing her, won't we, everybody? See you at the same time next week. This is Alan de Souza saying be good to each other and goodbye.' He bowed, flashed the teeth and waved.

There was more deafening applause, whistles and stamping of feet.

De Souza continued to wave and smile until he could see through the corner of his eye a monitor that showed that his picture was no longer being transmitted and the screen was now filled with a rolling list of the crew. Then the smile left him, and he ambled off the set.

As the racket lessened, the continuity announcer, a man in a glass cubicle said, 'That was another edition of *Wanna*

Be Rich? with Britain's most popular quiz master, Alan de Souza, direct and live from Leeds. Tune in at the same time next week and see what happens when Alan de Souza asks the ordinary man or woman in the street, "Wanna be rich?"' Recorded music swelled up and there was more deafening applause, whistles and stamping of feet encouraged by a smiling man in a red suit holding up a big card with the word 'Applause' printed on it. The noise faded out and the live transmission was over. Up came an advertisement for corn plasters.

A young woman was standing by a small trolley waiting for de Souza in the wings. She smiled and said, 'Great show, Alan.' Then she quickly unclipped a microphone from the presenter's jacket, took a battery and wire from his pocket, removed his earpiece and put them all on the trolley.

'Thank you,' de Souza said with a smile. 'It *did* seem to go rather well.'

She then passed him a glass of water with ice and a slice of lemon. He took a sip and handed it back.

'You get better each show, Alan. I'm sure you do,' she said as she handed him a small aerosol inhaler. De Souza put it up to his mouth, pressed the button and inhaled the vapour for a couple of seconds.

'You're very kind, Marie,' de Souza said as he returned the inhaler.

She fluttered her eyelids a couple of times and passed him a towel. 'No, it's true,' she said. 'You do.'

De Souza took the towel, wiped his mouth and hands, tossed the towel back across the woman's arm, smiled and said, 'Thank you, Marie.'

She smiled warmly.

Then de Souza quickly made his way along the narrow corridor towards the steps to the gallery from where the show's director had been controlling operations. He passed the floor manager, a big, smiling young man called Jed Morrison, who said, 'Another great show, Mr de Souza.'

De Souza smiled back at him.

'Sorry about the girls being a bit late with the flowers,' Morrison said. 'They were in position but they weren't watching me. They were busy watching you and the contestant.'

'I don't think anybody noticed, Jed. It was only a second or so.'

'I hear a few seconds out there seems like hours,' Morrison said, then pulled a face. 'I was balled out by Dennis Grant.'

'Don't worry about it,' de Souza said. 'Excuse me, Jed. Must dash.'

He reached the steps up to the gallery and took them two at a time.

Five young men and women were still at their desks in headphones in front of banks of switches and controls. They were closing down the cameras, autocues, microphones, recorder and lights. The programme director, Dennis Grant, stood up, took his coat from behind his chair and put it on.

'Thank you, everybody,' Grant said. 'Good night.'

'Night, Dennis,' they said.

As Grant made for the door, de Souza came in.

Grant looked at him and said, 'Oh. I was trying to get away before you showed up.'

'Great show,' de Souza said.

'You *thought* so? It wasn't from where I was sitting,' he said. 'It was a slack, slovenly performance from start to finish. Every single cue was late. The girls still haven't learned to get on fast, hand over the flowers and get off as quickly as possible. I tell you, it hasn't got the zing . . . the punch that American shows have.'

'Everything was fine, Dennis. Believe me. I didn't notice a thing. It was a great show. You worry too much.'

'That's kind of you, Alan,' he said, 'considering you are at the sharp end. If it's good, you get all the credit, and if anything goes wrong, you've got to stand there with egg on your face and take it. Wouldn't be at all surprised if you don't get an offer from the other side of the pond. In fact, you may already have had one.'

Dennis Grant stared closely at him. Alan de Souza smiled confidently back.

Grant said, 'You're not going to accept it, are you, Alan?'

De Souza continued to smile.

'You wouldn't, would you?' Grant said. 'After all Viktor has done for you?'

'Huh. He is only filling his wallet, Dennis. I mean nothing to him.'

'It was Viktor Berezin who gave you your first break.'

'He didn't do me any favours. There were many reasons why I got the job. Mostly luck. I was in the right place at the right time with the right amount of experience, having just finished that other series, and on contract, at the time, to Zenith Television. It was convenient, that's all. Nobody thought the show would be a hit like this, did they?'

Jed Morrison came up to them.

'Excuse me,' he said, then he looked at de Souza and said, 'Josephine Huxley is outside your dressing room waiting to see you.'

Grant waved his hand as if he was dismissing a slave. 'Mr de Souza is talking to *me*,' he said. 'She'll wait. She'll wait.'

'Thank you, Jed,' de Souza said. 'Please tell her I'll be along in a minute or so.'

'Right, Mr de Souza, thank you,' Morrison said, then he glared at Grant, turned and dashed off.

De Souza wasn't pleased. 'What is the matter with you, Dennis? You don't have to be so damned rude. Jed Morrison is a decent enough lad. He tries. He isn't a scrounger. And the contestant, Josephine Huxley, is a nice enough soul. And she performs well in front of the cameras, with a bit of encouragement, which I try to supply.'

'She doesn't need you to feed her ego,' Grant said. 'And we needn't worry about enrolling her sort of talent. There are thousands of stage-struck amateurs out there with photographic memories who can recall everything they read, and would do just about anything to get in front of a TV camera.'

'I daresay, Dennis, but it wouldn't do any harm to be encouraging.'

Grant breathed in slowly, his eyes like bilberries on stalks. When his chest was fully expanded, he said, 'You don't understand the priorities of this business. There's not a bloody professional among the lot of you.'

He went out and slammed the door.

Detective Inspector Michael Angel's office, Bromersley Police Station, South Yorkshire
Monday, 11 November 2013, 8.28 a.m.

As he came past the cells on the way to his office, Angel could hear a phone in the distance ringing insistently. It was not until he was walking down the corridor that he realized that it was *his* phone. He increased his speed, pushed open the office door, reached over the desk and snatched up the handpiece.

'Yes? Angel,' he said.

It was Sergeant Clifton from the control office. 'An anonymous triple nine has just come in from a call box out at the bottom of Dog's Leg Hill, sir. Car gone through a stone wall halfway down. Caller said the driver looked in a bad way. I've sent an ambulance.'

Angel nodded and said, 'I'll go, Bernie. Put a call out for DS Carter to join me when she arrives.'

He replaced the phone and dashed out into the corridor. He met Flora Carter as she was making her way into the CID room.

'Flora, come with me. There's a triple nine. We'll go in my car.'

In five minutes, they arrived at the top of the hill where stood Abercrombie Hall, an imposing stone-built house with large grounds and an envious view towards the Pennines. They turned there on to Dog's Leg Hill and found themselves behind an ambulance that clearly was making for the same destination. Angel did not choose to overtake it. There were no pedestrians or traffic about but the ambulance had its lights flashing and its siren blaring. It managed to scare a couple of magpies away. It took the hill at a steady fifteen to twenty miles an hour and stopped at the hole in the wall.

The two men rushed out of the ambulance carrying bags. Angel and Flora Carter followed quickly, picking their way carefully over what was left standing of the stone wall.

They saw the car, buckled up against the tree. The driver's door was wide open but there was nobody inside. They looked round.

Angel spotted a light brown coat, a pair of legs, feet and women's shoes about twenty yards from the car wreck. It was the figure of a slim woman near some brambles, half hidden by long grass. She was in a foetal position, her slim hands palm downward across her stomach. There were no rings on her fingers or watch on her wrist.

'Over here,' he said. 'Looks as if she managed to climb out of the car and get here before collapsing.'

The ambulance men dropped on to their knees and began the examination. One of them put a stethoscope on to her chest. The other touched her neck, looked up at Angel and said, 'She's very cold.'

After a few seconds, the other pulled the stethoscope off his ears and said, 'There's nothing there. She's gone.'

Then there was that inevitable moment of silence, like a spell, as the three men and the woman absorbed the enormity of the loss of a life, as one would do at the birth of a *new* life.

The ambulance men were the first to move.

Angel said, 'Is she beyond the possibility of being revived?'

'Well past,' one of the men said. 'She's very cold.'

'Right. Leave her there then. She can go in the mortuary van, after SOCO have seen her.'

'Righto,' the spokesman said, and they set about packing up their gear.

Angel went over to the wrecked car, which was impacted into the tree. The front of it had concertinaed into about three-quarters its length, and the steering wheel was only about ten inches from the driver's seat. Most of the windows were shattered and there was blood on the upholstery and the seat belt.

There was a handbag on the driver's seat. The contents were strewn about the navy-blue upholstery. He looked for a wallet or purse. There was neither, nor were there any keys. He looked at the car's ignition. The car key was in position, and there were several other keys hanging down on the ring.

He rubbed his chin then swiftly turned to Flora Carter and said, 'Get SOCO out here smartly, Flora. And we'd better get our transport department to look at this car urgently. Tell Martin Edwards I want him here in ten minutes, and tell him I don't want any faffing about.'

'Right, sir,' she said. She stabbed her finger on the pad of her mobile and then put it to her ear. She looked at Angel and said, 'Something the matter, sir?'

He pursed his lips. 'Aye. She's been robbed,' he said.

Flora Carter looked shocked. 'Huh?' she said.

Angel quickly added, 'Take the car reg and find out the name and address of the owner. I'll just have a look round . . .'

He wandered off thoughtfully, across a small paddock of grass spotted with several trees and brambles. He saw something shining. It was a small empty whisky bottle. He managed to poke it towards his feet with a twig. The screw cap was missing. He bent down, stuck the end of the twig into the top and lifted it up to look at it. The bottle wasn't dirty and it didn't look as if it had been there long. He carried it like this, carefully clambering over the damaged wall to his car. He opened the boot, found an evidence bag large enough, then carefully slid the bottle in and sealed it.

Meanwhile the ambulance men had loaded their gear and were on their way back up Dog's Leg Hill.

DS Carter came up to him. 'I spoke to Don Taylor, sir. SOCO on their way. And Martin Edwards said he'd be here in ten minutes. He said should he bring a low loader. I said yes.'

Angel nodded. 'Good.'

'The owner of the car is a Jeni Lowe of The Cottage, Frog Lane. That's further along Long Lane towards the moors, about a mile. Frog Lane is on the map but it must be very narrow. Do you want me to go?'

He wrinkled his nose. He didn't fancy breaking the news to her family or whoever she lived with, but he believed it was part of his job. 'I'll go.'

'We could do with some uniformed to attend here, sir.'

'Aye. Ring the control room. We shall need them until the car has been recovered and SOCO has completed a full search of the field.'

TWO

Frog Lane, Bromersley, South Yorkshire
Monday, 11 November 2013, 10.00 a.m.

Angel pointed the bonnet of the BMW along Long Lane, the narrow bottom road away from town. He passed a small single-storey stone-built house on the corner on his left. Unusually, he saw smoke issuing out of the chimney. He turned on to a narrower road, which was Frog Lane. A few hundred metres down there was a small house on the left that had the sign 'The Cottage' fastened to the front gate. It had a small front garden and double gates to a very short drive, which led to a wooden garage erected at the side of the house. He looked up at the windows. They seemed to be intact; that was a good sign. He went up the little path to the front door and banged the knocker several times. There was no reply. He banged the knocker again. He stood back from the door and sighed, then went round to the back of the house. He was not surprised to see a downstairs window hanging open. The glass in the window had been smashed.

He peered through the window into a small kitchen. Cupboard doors were wide open. The drawer in the sink unit was pulled out. Tins and packets of groceries, pots and cutlery were strewn around. Some packets had been opened and the contents spilled on the worktops and floor.

Angel's lips tightened back against his teeth. Sadly, he had seen houses of murdered people practically pulled to pieces before, having been rigorously searched to remove any reference or clue that might identify the murderer. It was wicked, evil and monstrous, but it happened.

Angel reached into his pocket for his mobile.

Ten minutes later, a police car dropped off a uniformed constable at The Cottage.

Angel was waiting for him at the kitchen window. He pointed to it and said, 'Somebody has gained access there, lad. There's a possibility that the intruder is still inside, so keep your eye on it. SOCO will be down later to go over the place. All right?'

'Right, sir,' he said.

Angel returned to the BMW. It was warmer in the car out of the wind. He took out his mobile to speak to Flora Carter.

'Flora,' he said. 'I'm still here at The Cottage. It *has* been broken into. Tell Don Taylor that when he has finished there I want him and his team to check over this place.'

'Right, sir,' she said. 'I'm glad you've rung. DS Martin Edwards wants a word. He's here.'

Angel blinked. 'Put him on, Flora.'

Edwards took over the phone and said, 'I thought you'd want to know, sir, that there is brake fluid all over the place underneath this car. On closer examination I found that one of the car's brake cables has been severed with a serrated blade.'

'Do you mean a hacksaw?'

'Probably a hacksaw, sir. Whatever it was, it couldn't be accidental, it *has* to be deliberate.'

Angel blew out a yard of air, then heavily said, 'Right, Martin. Thank you for that. Put me back to Flora.'

'I'm here, sir,' she said. 'I heard what Martin said.'

'Well, you'll know the significance of *that* then, Flora. I'm going to call on the other house down here so I'll be a little while yet.'

Angel reflected for a moment that he was now *definitely* investigating a case of murder, then he shoved his mobile phone determinedly into his pocket, sighed, started the car, and headed for the house on Long Lane.

As he pulled up outside the front of the house, he noticed a sign screwed to the grey stone wall: 'The Bailiff's House.' Beneath the sign, against the wall, was a wooden packing case. The case was set on what looked like old pram wheels, and it had a piece of rope fastened to it in two places to enable it to be towed around like a box cart.

He made his way up to the front door and banged on the knocker. While he was waiting, he peered inside the box cart. He could see small pieces of coal, coal dust and fragments of dead twigs. Nobody answered the door. He was about to bang again when a grey-haired man peered round the corner of the house.

'What do you want, old chap?' the man said.

Angel's eyebrows shot up. An elderly man with a military moustache was shuffling along in a pair of woolly slippers. He had an accent that seemed very much out of place in the backwoods of a South Yorkshire village.

Angel pulled out his ID and said, 'I'm Detective Inspector Angel, Bromersley police. Can I have a word with you, sir?'

'Of course. Of course. Come on in. Put that away, old chap. I can't see the damned thing anyway. I haven't got my glasses. Follow me. We'll go in the back door, if you don't mind. Don't know where the key to that front door is anyway. Lost it ages ago.'

Angel followed him along the path at the side of the little house to the back door.

'Well, well, well. A policeman, are you? We don't see many bobbies down here. You must be freezing. Come inside. You'll have a cup of tea or coffee?'

'No, thank you, sir.'

'Oh dear, oh dear. Can't have that, old chap. I make a good cup of tea. I'm afraid I can't offer you anything stronger. Ran out last night. I've nothing warmer till the damned shop delivers, you know.'

Angel looked round the cosy, tiny kitchen. He particularly enjoyed the big red glowing fire in the black kitchen range.

'Sit down, old chap. Don't stand on ceremony. Now what is it all about?'

'Can I have your name, sir?'

'Antony Edward Abercrombie, sir. Used to live in the hall up the road, you know.'

Angel pursed his lips. 'What, Abercrombie Hall?'

'That's the one. Exactly. I was born there. So was my father, my grandfather and even before that, but some chap came along and my father did some deal with him and then suddenly died — my father I mean — and the bums came in and put me out. I've lived here ever since. I have to pay rent for this little hen coop to the Abercrombie estate. I thought *I* was the Abercrombie estate, but in the eyes of the law, I'm not. Different entity altogether. But look here, old chap. You didn't come here to listen to me rabbiting on. What did you want?'

Angel wanted to get on. 'Last night, sir, did you see or hear anything unusual happening round here?'

'No. I sleep like a log. Wouldn't hear Niagara Falls, old chap. No. Like a log. Why?'

'A young woman who lives near here crashed her car through a wall and died.'

Abercrombie's eyebrows went up. 'Really? Dashed awful, I say. Damned dashed awful. Oh dear. Must have been at the bottom of Dog's Leg Hill. Hellish hill, that.'

'You know nothing?'

'No. Like a log, you know. Who was she? Do I know her?'

'Jeni Lowe.'

Abercrombie looked down at his feet in thought. He shook his head and said, 'Jeni Lowe. Not unless it's that filly from The Cottage?'

'You knew her?'

'No, old chap. Seen her pass by here in a little runabout. Wished I was fifty years younger, what? Oh dear. Very sad.'

'Can you tell me anything about her at all?'

'No, old chap, sorry. Pretty little thing. Not a clue. Very sad.'

'She was also robbed,' Angel said.

Abercrombie's eyes nearly popped out of his head. 'Robbed? Oh, I say, that's damned bad form. Not the ticket at all.' He shook his head. 'Disgraceful. It's the discipline that's lacking. Both with their parents and then at school. They were heavy with the stick when I was at school, Inspector. Didn't do me any harm. I hope you catch the blackguards.'

Angel nodded. 'I'll do my best. You can't help me then, Mr Abercrombie?'

'Sorry, old chap. No. That's a bad show. Awful.'

'Very well,' Angel said, getting to his feet.

'Don't go, Inspector. I wish I had a bottle of something so that I could offer you a drink but I am afraid this house is as dry as a nun's wimple.'

'No. No, Mr Abercrombie,' Angel said with a smile. 'That's all right. By the way, for the record, where were you between nine o'clock last night and six o'clock this morning?'

Abercrombie's jaw dropped. 'I don't know, old chap. Here and there, you know. Most of the time I'd be in bed, I suppose. But I'd go here and there.'

Angel frowned and turned to look at him. 'Here and there?' he said.

'Yes, well, at my age and living on my own, I might go from one room to another to see something or fetch something, and when I get there, I've forgotten what I've gone there for. Then again I might feel like a shower. I spend a lot of time in the bathroom. Or a drink of tea. The kitchen. I go where I damned well please. Why not? Eh?'

'I meant, did you leave the house between those times?'

Abercrombie screwed up his face in thought, then he smiled. 'I see what you mean, old chap,' he said. 'Ah. It's the alibi thing, isn't it? Yes. No. No. After dark I am always in this house with the door locked until daylight in the morning.'

'Thank you very much. And the barrow outside the front . . . what do you use that for?'

'Transport, old chap. Don't have a car. The bums took the damned thing from me. Got to have it delivered or I go out and get it. Wheels, you know. Got to have wheels.'

Angel took his leave and returned to the scene of the car accident. He parked the BMW behind SOCO's van and four other police cars.

DS Donald Taylor, in charge of SOCO, saw him arrive and approached him.

'We've finished here, sir. We've gone over this field thoroughly and there's nothing fresh that we could reliably use as evidence.'

'I understand that, Don,' Angel said. 'Have you found any man-made prints of any kind, or animal prints?'

'No human prints, sir. A few old hoof prints in the frozen mud by the gate, nothing else.'

Angel wrinkled his nose. It was disappointing. 'I have an empty whisky bottle I found among the brambles earlier. I'll let you have it. There'll be prints on that.'

Taylor's face brightened. 'Right, sir. That's good. We are moving straight on to The Cottage now, sir.'

Angel nodded. 'I'll be along there later.'

Taylor nodded and went back towards the SOCO van.

Angel turned away as Flora Carter approached him.

'I've been thinking, sir,' she said. 'Do you think the victim was carrying something valuable in the car? Something that thieves or a thief wanted?'

Angel frowned. 'You mean they fixed the brakes, followed the car, waited for it to crash, then stole the item from her?'

'Something like that.'

'Sounds possible, Flora, but she's only a slightly built young woman. Why not simply push her out of the way and take it? Why kill her? There must be half a dozen different ways of taking something valuable away from her without killing her.'

'Maybe they didn't expect that fixing the brakes would result in her death?'

'Maybe not but you wouldn't fix somebody's brakes in that way if you wanted them to live a long and happy life, would you?'

'I suppose not, sir.'

'Whoever fixed her brakes, Flora, wanted her dead or at least afraid for her life. Martin Edwards says that it couldn't be accidental, therefore it was deliberate. That means it was murder.'

It was three o'clock before Angel returned to his office from Dog's Leg Hill, resigned to the fact that SOCO had not found any forensic at the scene of crime that would be helpful to the investigation. The SOCO team had moved on to The Cottage, home of the victim, and he was hopeful of finding a fruitful line of inquiry that he could follow while the trail was fresh.

He slumped down in the swivel chair and picked up his phone. He tapped in a number and sighed heavily as he waited for a response.

'Ah, Mac,' he said. 'You have the body of a young woman there who, I understand, died from a motor accident late yesterday or early today. Her name we now know is Jeni Lowe. What can you tell me?'

'Jeni Lowe, is it?' Mac said. 'Well, I have started on her, Michael. I knew it wouldn't be long before you would start chivvying me. She seems to have died from a loss of blood due principally to a fresh wound on her chest but she also has a fresh wound on her head. Both wounds as a result of the accident, I believe.'

'Have you got the time of death, Mac?'

'Yes. I have taken a greater margin on this, Michael, because of two unknown factors: the ambient temperature and the strength of the wind. I believe that it was cold but not freezing, and that there was little or no wind. So I reckon she must have died sometime between nine o'clock last night and three o'clock this morning.'

'Right, Mac, thank you.'

Angel terminated the call and rang Martin Edwards, the sergeant in charge of the station vehicles.

'Michael Angel here. Is there anything new to tell me about the young woman's car, Martin?'

'Yes, sir. There are lots of fingerprints inside it, sir. They might prove useful.'

Angel was looking for anything fresh that might point him in the direction of a specific line of inquiry.

'Send those prints on to SOCO as soon as you can,' he said. 'Are there any prints on the braking system that might help us to support the case that it had been tampered with?'

'No, sir. We won't be able to get any prints from anywhere around there. The system is heavily covered in the brake oil. However I can remove the damaged pipes which clearly show the marks where the saw had been used.'

'Great stuff. It will show that the car had been interfered with. Did you find anything useful in the boot or in the dashboard pockets?'

'Only what you would expect.'

Angel was disappointed. 'All right,' he said. 'Be sure to let me know straightaway if you find anything unusual or different. I need some leads and quick, Martin.'

He replaced the phone.

He could have thrown it at the wall but instead he tapped in Don's number.

'Are you on with that house on Frog Lane, Don?'

'Yes, sir, and it's a hell of a mess,' Taylor said. 'Packets of sugar and flour and stuff like that have been opened and scattered around.'

Angel rubbed his chin. 'Have you finished your sweep for prints and so on?'

'Almost. Another few minutes.'

'I'll come straight down.'

Paul Rose was a little exasperated. 'Oh, Helen,' he said, as he washed his hands in the kitchen sink at The Brambles, 'you don't want to take any notice of what Cora says. She's not very bright and will repeat any old tale that's going round.'

'But it's *history,* Paul,' Helen Rose said, holding out her hands for emphasis. 'It happened here, in this house.'

'Well, people have to be born, live their lives and die *somewhere*, haven't they? You could say every house has history, but I am sure that *that* history is not re-enacted time after time after time. What would be the point?'

'But this is an *old* house, Paul. It is full of *old* history.'

'What's the age of a house got to do with it?' he said, reaching out for a towel. 'I was brought up in an old house but there weren't any spirits mooching around there. Look, Helen, this house was supposed to have been built in the mid-eighteenth century, that's 1750, isn't it? It will have been lived in by many families since then. I remember the solicitor said that the vendor and his family lived here twenty-two years. They must have been happy enough. No spooky stories about drunken sex-mad dentists and cattle slaughterers seem to have bothered them.'

Helen Rose shuddered. 'Ever since Cora told me all that,' she said, 'when I'm in the house on my own, I feel nervous. Every creak of a floorboard or any inexplicable noise and I freeze up. I can't help it.'

'All houses make noises, sweetheart. The last house I lived in made a sort of cracking noise occasionally. My father used to say, "They're settling noises. Take no notice." And we didn't.'

'But I don't think the story is fiction, darling,' she said.

'It might not be, but the point is why would the Cudlipp family manifest themselves after all this time? That's assuming you believe in ghosts. They haven't the ability to harm you, so what are you worrying about?'

'Well, I don't believe in ghosts like spooky things running about in white sheets, but I do believe in the possibility of the spirits of people, particularly our loved ones who have died, being . . . around us, particularly in times of crisis, or when we have to make a momentous decision, and decidedly at the time of our death.'

'Who knows?' Paul Rose said. 'You might be right. But, even if you *are*, you're not anticipating the Cudlipps doing you any harm, are you?'

'I suppose not, but . . . I can't help . . . I can't help how I feel.'

THREE

Angel stopped the BMW outside Jeni Lowe's little house on Frog Lane, parking up behind SOCO's white van. He acknowledged the salute of a uniformed constable on the front door, rang the bell and tried the door. It was unlocked so he went inside into a small hallway.

A man dressed from head to toe in white and wearing a linen mask over his mouth and nose peered out of a room into the little hall.

It was Don Taylor. 'Oh, it's you, sir,' he said.

'Do I need gloves, lad?' Angel said.

'Got some here, sir,' he said, taking a paper packet out of his top pocket and handing it to him.

Angel tore open the paper wrapping and began pulling on the gloves. 'What have you got then, Don?'

'Nothing specific yet, sir. We've vacuumed everywhere, and we've swabbed all the access points, light switches, the lifting points on furniture, ornaments, pictures and the like. We've just started looking at the contents of the cupboards and—'

Angel blew out a yard of air. 'Have you found out anything about *her*?' he said.

'Yes. She's clean, methodical, hasn't much but what she's got is good quality.'

Angel said, 'Yes, Don, but have you discovered where she works, who her friends are, who her next of kin is, or who her husband, boyfriend, partner or sugar daddy is?'

'No, sir. But there are no signs of a man living or having lived with her here.'

Angel's eyes opened wide, displaying white all round the pupil. 'Really? That *is* surprising these days,' he said, shaking his head.

He wandered into the hall. A moment later he returned. 'Where's her phone?'

'She doesn't seem to have one, sir.'

'Strange,' Angel said. He rubbed his chin.

'There's a drawer in the sideboard, sir. It has her passport and NHS card and other bits and pieces in it. All that ID gen might be in there.'

'Oh good. Show me.'

Taylor showed Angel into the living room, which was small but cosy. He was led to a sideboard, where Taylor pulled out a shallow drawer and put it on the table behind them. Angel sat down and began fingering through the few documents that were there.

He saw that Jeni Lowe's passport had her occupation down as a copywriter. There was a building society book that indicated that she had a mortgage with them and was making monthly repayments by standing order from the Northern Bank. There were bank statements dated 2010 in a plastic binder giving an address in Nottingham. There was nothing else in the drawer. He had expected her cheque book at least being there. He took possession of the documents and returned the drawer to the sideboard. Then he pulled out his mobile and phoned DS Crisp.

The recorded voice on Crisp's mobile directed him to voicemail as so often it did. Angel made an angry exclamation and cancelled the call.

DS Trevor Crisp was one of the two sergeants on his team. He was in his thirties, and a regular Romeo. Women liked him but he never seemed to develop a long-standing relationship with any of them.

Angel considered him to be a handsome philanderer, who could charm monkeys out of the trees, and occasionally he had put Crisp in situations where he had used that charm to progress inquiries in difficult cases. He was also adept at keeping out of the way, particularly when there was work to be done.

Angel pulled out his mobile and scrolled down his contacts to Ahmed Ahaz.

'Is DS Crisp there, lad?'

Ahmed looked round the CID room. 'Can't see him, sir. He's not here.'

'Find him, Ahmed. I've got a job for him. Find him. And have him phone me ASAP.'

'Right, sir.'

Angel stuffed the phone into his pocket.

Something was bothering him. He walked up and down the room several times, frowned and ran his hand through his hair. Then he stopped, stood still and rubbed his chin. He turned to Taylor and said, 'Are you *sure* you haven't come across Jeni Lowe's mobile phone?'

'No, sir. I didn't know she had one.'

Angel pursed his lips briefly then said, 'She was *bound* to have one. She hasn't a landline. She was under thirty and not short of a few bob.'

'Well, it's not here, sir.'

The following morning was Tuesday, 12 November.

Angel reached his office at 8.28 a.m. as usual. He picked up the phone. 'Ahmed,' he said. 'When DS Crisp comes in, don't forget, I want to see him.'

'I know, sir,' Ahmed said. 'I hadn't forgotten.'

'And let me have the CID copy of Yellow Pages covering South Yorkshire.'

'Right, sir.'

Ahmed brought in the phone book and rushed out.

Angel turned to Advertising Agencies. There were only two: J.S.P. Tollemache Limited and The Meyer Agency. They were both in Sheffield. He phoned them and discovered that Jeni Lowe worked for The Meyer Agency, that she had been missing from work yesterday and that they had not heard from her, which was very unlike her. Angel didn't explain but made an arrangement to call on the creative director, Harry Khan, her immediate boss, later that day. He replaced the phone and rubbed his chin. He was thinking about what he needed to do next when there was a knock on his door.

'Come in.'

It was DS Crisp. 'Good morning, sir. I understand you've been looking for me.'

Angel stared at him. He could feel rage bubbling in his chest and rising to his face. 'Where the hell have you been? I've been trying to get you since yesterday afternoon.'

Crisp smiled uncertainly.

Angel said, 'In the meantime we're in the throes of an investigation into the murder of a young woman. Absolutely nothing is more important than that at this time.'

'Yes, sir. I'm up to speed on it. I've read the report.'

'Now, I've warned you, Crisp, more than once, about you switching your mobile off in working hours.'

'I think it must be faulty, sir.'

'Well, get it checked out.'

'Right, sir.'

'Now let's get on with some work. I want you to find out who lives at that Nottingham address on Jeni Lowe's 2011 bank statements. We need her next of kin, but more importantly we need to know the names and addresses of her circle of friends and relations, and most importantly the menfolk in her life.'

'Right, sir,' he said.

He stood up and rushed off.

Angel watched the door close. He sniffed and shook his head.

He reached out for the phone and tapped in Flora Carter's mobile number.

'Where are you, lass?'

'CID office, sir,' Flora Carter said.

'Pop across. I've got a job for you.'

Two minutes later, there was a knock on the door. Flora Carter came in and closed the door.

'Sit down,' he said. 'I want you to go to the Northern Bank.'

He swivelled round to the small table behind his chair and picked up a black plastic folder. It was a Northern Bank issue statement cover.

'Here are Jeni Lowe's bank statements,' he said, passing it to her. 'They go back to 2011. See what you can find out about her: who she pays out to and what for. See if she buys anything unusual. And see if she buys anything for a man. We need to find the man in her life.'

Leaning her head to one side, Flora said, 'Have you never thought, sir, in these enlightened days, that Jeni Lowe might have a *partner*?'

Angel looked into Flora's mischievous eyes. 'Well, whatever it is, Flora, whether it's animal, mineral or vegetable, I want to know about it.'

Angel stopped the BMW at 9.55 a.m. outside a new tall building in the middle of Sheffield. It looked as if it had been built with aluminium, glass and bathroom tiles. He saw a sign that invited visitors to use the company car park. It directed him to drive through a short tunnel in the building and then down a steep narrow slope to a barrier in the basement. He drove up to the bar across the road and a white-haired man dressed in a black uniform not dissimilar to a standard police uniform came out of a kiosk.

As he leaned forward, Angel lowered the car window.

The man said, 'Good morning, sir. Who did you want to see?'

'Harry Khan at The Meyer Agency. He is expecting me. My name is Inspector Angel.'

The man peered back at him and smiled. 'Did you say Inspector Angel, sir? Are you Detective Inspector *Michael* Angel?'

Angel's eyebrows shot up. 'Why, yes, I am.'

The man smiled broadly. 'Well, well, well,' he said. 'I was reading about you in the paper recently. It was about that case where you discovered that the crooks in the town had a cuckoo clock, and *that* helped you to find a murderer and bring him back from Switzerland. Fantastic. You're the detective who always gets his man, aren't you? Huh! Like the Mounties. You're on the Bromersley force, sir, aren't you? Eeee, wait while I tell my missus I've met you.'

Angel smiled. He waited while the torrent ceased. 'Do you think I could see Mr Khan, please?'

The man smiled. 'Of course, sir. You must excuse me. We don't see many celebrities on this job, you know.'

He went back into the kiosk, reached for the phone, pressed several keys, muttered something into the mouth-piece, waited, then replaced the phone, came out of the kiosk and said, 'Right, Inspector. Drive straight on, park up in any marked-out space, then take the lift to the second floor to Mr Khan's office, room 207.'

'Thank you,' Angel said, and followed the attendant's directions.

Harry Khan stood up. 'Come in, Inspector Angel.' He shook his hand firmly. 'Please sit down. Can I offer you coffee or tea . . . or anything?'

'Nothing, thank you,' Angel said.

'Make yourself comfortable and tell me what's happened to Jeni Lowe. Whatever has happened that requires a police inspector to visit us?'

'You are Jeni Lowe's immediate boss?'

'Yes, Inspector. I am the creative director. She worked in the studio with the rest of the creative team. What's going on?'

'Jeni Lowe met with a tragic accident. Her car went through a stone wall and hit a tree. We discovered that her brakes had been interfered with. She died shortly afterwards. We are treating the case as murder.'

Harry Khan's mouth dropped open.

'I need to know who her closest friends were,' Angel continued. 'In particular the name of anyone who was a close friend or partner?'

Khan looked down and shook his head. 'It's unbelievable. She was such a nice young woman.'

'Please tell me what you know about her.'

'Oh dear, oh dear, oh dear,' Khan said.

'I know it's a shock. Tell me, in your own time.'

'Yes, well. Er, thank you. She came here in answer to an ad for a copywriter about five years ago. I interviewed her. She had no experience of working in an agency. I gave her and the other two candidates briefing for an ad, and a half hour to do the best they could with it. She produced the best copy by far, so she got the job. Since then, she's just been great. Pleasant, reliable and so on. She had bizarre ideas and an uncommon and colourful imagination. She understood business. She was also very presentable to clients. Not all arty people are, you know.'

'You mean she was attractive?'

'That as well. Let's face it, Inspector, everybody loves beautiful people. And generally speaking, a smart, pretty woman will sell more cars to men than men, and a handsome hunk of a man will always sell more gowns and groceries to women than women. It's a fact.'

'It's sex.'

'Absolutely, and Jeni Lowe often accompanied the account executive to clients' offices. She has accompanied me on some occasions. It's tragic. She'll be very sadly missed.'

'Did she strike up a special relationship with anybody else here?'

Khan pursed his lips. 'She was popular with everybody, as far as I know.'

'Where did she actually work?'

‘She had a desk in the studio, with the other members of the team. Would you like to see it?’

‘I certainly would. And I would also like to meet her workmates.’

‘Of course,’ Khan said. He stood up. ‘Follow me. They are all very busy just now, with deadlines to meet.’

Khan opened a door opposite the one Angel had entered through, which led directly into a studio which was set out like a schoolroom. There were eight designers’ desks with a young man or woman stood or seated behind each one, and two writing desks with computers standing on them. They were all facing a large blackboard that occupied the entire wall.

Angel noticed that one of the writing desks was unattended.

Khan addressed the group. He told them that Jeni Lowe was dead and how she had died. There was shock and tears from the group. He explained who Angel was, then said, ‘The inspector wants to ask you a few questions.’

Khan then waved a hand in Angel’s direction.

Angel said, ‘Thank you, Mr Khan.’ He turned to the group and said, ‘Please gather round. It’s possible you can help me. Do you know of any person who might have wanted to frighten — or as it has sadly resulted, murder — Jeni Lowe?’

‘Oh no,’ they all said.

‘It must have been someone who is sick,’ a young woman in a T-shirt and jeans said.

The rest of the group showed or muttered their agreement.

Angel nodded then said, ‘Has any one of you had, or were having, a special relationship with her?’

‘No,’ they all said.

One young man, with a diamond stud in his ear and tattoos appearing through the banana-yellow collar of his shirt, said, ‘I took her out once. She was absolutely lovely but we didn’t quite hit it off. I was interested in music and having a few drinks but she could only talk about work, and she didn't like modern music or drinking very much either.'

'Thank you for that,' Angel said.

'But she was good fun at the Christmas party,' another man said.

Angel turned back to the group and said, 'Does anybody know if she had a person with whom she had a special relationship?'

A young woman said, 'Quite recently she said that she had to get home quickly after work because she had a date with a man who she was keen on.'

Another young woman said, 'She told *me* that. Poor Jeni.'

'But did she mention his name or indicate anything that might help identify him?' Angel said.

'No. She didn't to me, anyway. But she had certainly got the hots for him.'

Angel nodded. 'Well, thank you for that, everybody,' he said. 'Just one more thing. Does anybody have Jeni's mobile number?'

'Yeah, sure.' The young man with the tattoos checked the list on his mobile and wrote it down on a scrap of paper.

'Thank you,' Angel said, and stuffed it into his wallet. Then he said, 'Has anybody any idea where she might have been on Sunday evening? We think she was travelling home when the crash happened, but we have no idea where she had been.'

Nobody replied. Nobody seemed to know.

'Right, thank you. Now lastly, if any of you can think of any reason why anyone would want to murder her, please let me know. I'll leave my phone number with Mr Khan. We *have* to find her murderer. Thank you very much.'

With that, he turned to Khan and said, 'Thank you for letting me talk to them.'

Khan nodded and turned to the group. 'All right, girls and boys,' he said.

They returned to their working stations in silence.

Angel said, 'That computer on the desk at the back, Mr Khan . . . the one that is unattended. Was that Jeni Lowe's place?'

'Yes.'

'I'd like to look through that desk, Mr Khan. And I'll need to borrow that computer tower.'

Khan gestured with his hands that Angel should do what he had to do.

Angel quickly made his way between the designers' desks to the back of the room and looked through the two drawers. There was a part pack of A4 white paper and a notebook in the top drawer, and a giant dictionary and thesaurus in the other.

He slammed shut the drawers and blew out a length of air. He thought a moment then pulled open the top drawer again. He reached inside and took out the notebook. It was open at a blank page. He flicked through the book. All the pages were blank on both sides. Clearly Jeni Lowe had torn out the used pages and disposed of them as they had become no longer useful. Angel found the front cover of the notebook with the stationer's name and address printed on it. There were also, in blue ballpoint, several doodles of the curly-whirly type that Jeni might have done when engaged in a phone call. Angel then noticed something he thought very significant. In the top left-hand corner of the cover, in very neat handwriting, she had written:

Jeni Lowe

Miss Jeni Lowe

Viktor Berezin and Jeni Berezin

Mrs V. Berezin

Angel rubbed his chin. His pulse quickened and his chest felt as if spring had come, even though it was November. Who was Viktor Berezin? He had heard the name somewhere. He asked Khan and the men and women in the creative department but nobody knew. Anyway, Angel had a lead. Find Viktor Berezin.

FOUR

It was twelve noon before Angel returned to his office. He dropped Jeni's notebook on his desk, picked up the phone and tapped in SOCO's number.

Don Taylor answered.

'Don,' Angel said. 'I want you to pick up a computer from The Meyer Agency in Sheffield. It was regularly used by Jeni Lowe. I want you to see what you can find on it.'

'Right, sir. We'll give it a thorough search.'

'Good. And while you're on, have you heard of a man called Viktor Berezin?'

There was a knock at the door.

'No, sir. Sounds foreign to me. Czech or Romania, that sort of country.'

'Just a minute, Don,' Angel said, then he put his hand over the mouthpiece of the phone and called out, 'Come in.'

Flora Carter opened the door. Seeing him on the phone, she hesitated.

'It's all right. Sit down, Flora. Won't be long.'

He removed his hand from the mouthpiece. 'Yes, Don?' he said.

'No, sir. I haven't heard of Viktor Berezin,' Taylor said.

'If it comes to you, let me know,' Angel said.

He replaced the phone, turned to Flora and said, 'Now then, what did you find out at the bank?'

'Not much, sir,' Flora said. 'Jeni Lowe opened the account in Nottingham and it was transferred to the Bromersley branch last year. She has a small credit balance. Her salary is paid directly into her account. She makes a standing order to the building society every month. The payments she makes appear to be mostly by credit card for groceries, clothes and petrol. There are no unusual debits or credits from it. She manages her account properly and carefully. There's nothing else really to say.'

Angel wrinkled his nose. 'Hmm. Nothing *there* to help us then?'

Flora shook her head.

'Right. Moving on. Have you heard of a man called Viktor Berezin?'

'Sounds Russian, sir. Is he one of the oligarchy who have recently fled Russia?'

'Huh! So that Mr Putin doesn't get his hands on their roubles?' Angel said. 'I dunno, Flora. I really don't know.'

He picked up the notebook and pointed to the four short lines of neat handwriting on the front cover. 'It's a name that meant something to Jeni Lowe,' he said.

Flora Carter read them. She frowned. 'Yes, well,' she said. She flicked through the notebook to see if there was anything written inside, then she said, 'It certainly looks as if she had a dream, or . . . or an idea, or an expectation or anticipation of *some* sort.'

'That's exactly what I thought. We've got to find Viktor Berezin.'

Helen Rose was in the kitchen of The Brambles setting the table for supper. She looked up at the kitchen clock. She had looked at it a dozen or more times in the last five minutes. It was five o'clock. Paul wouldn't be home for another forty minutes or so. She would be overjoyed to see him.

Outside, the sky was as black as fingerprint ink, and a cold powerful wind began to blow from the east causing the trees and bushes in the garden at The Brambles to wave wildly in response.

Suddenly, from outside, a high piercing squeak of old dry metal hinges followed by the loud bang of a door came from the big stone outbuilding which stood twenty yards away from the back of the house.

The din was repeated. Again. And again.

Helen Rose's breathing quickened. She stood by the table motionless and listened as she tugged tight the teacloth she was holding between her hands. She remained there a minute or more. Then she suddenly charged over to the window, pulled open a curtain and peered out into the darkness. By cupping her eyes over the glass, to mask out the kitchen light, she could just make out that a door on the outbuilding was swinging free and taking quite a battering.

The old stone building had had many uses over the years. Originally it had been a slaughterhouse at one end and a stable and a place to house a carriage at the other, but latterly it had been a workshop, and a garage. The Roses only used the one end of it at the moment to garage the car that Paul took to work.

Helen rushed into the hall at the front of the house, grabbed her raincoat, put a headscarf on, took the chain off the back door and went out into the storm. The cold rain beat into her cheeks like pins fired from a battery of guns. She soon reached the garage door. It required a steady grip to wrestle against the wind to close it. But she managed and then dropped the latch. She turned round to make her way back to the house when suddenly she saw the silhouetted figure of a big broad-shouldered man wearing a stovepipe top hat about twenty feet away and coming towards her.

Her blood turned to water. Her heart pounded like a machine gun.

She screamed and turned to run.

Her legs were slow and heavy as lead, but she made it round the back of the outbuilding and down the drive towards the lane.

A vehicle was travelling along the lane from Bromersley and veered towards her. She was trapped in its lights like a hare. Terrified, she froze on the spot. The vehicle slowed down. It turned left up the drive and stopped at her side.

Its windscreen wipers were working hard and the rain flashed like silver wire in the headlights. Still panting, she saw that it was her husband, Paul Rose, in their car. She sighed with relief.

He lowered the car window. 'Darling! What's the matter? What are you doing out here?' he said. 'You're soaked. Get in the car.'

He drove up the drive and round to the outbuilding, garaged the car and the two of them went into the house.

After she had told him everything that had happened, he shook his head and said, 'Well, you're all right now, sweetheart. I couldn't do with anything happening to you. You'd better get into some dry clothes.'

She nodded and went upstairs, undoing her blouse buttons as she walked.

Paul Rose then went into the front hall and put on his most waterproof coat, hat and boots. He pocketed a rubber-cased torch then went outside into the storm. He returned a few minutes later as Helen came downstairs in her nightdress and housecoat.

When she saw him in his wet coat and carrying a hat, her eyes flashed. 'Oh, Paul,' she said. 'You've been out!'

He smiled gently at her. 'Just to see that everything was all right, sweetheart. Any tea?'

'Tea'll be five minutes. Well, er . . . what did you find?'

'Everything seems all right to me,' he said and turned towards the hall. 'I'll go and get ready.'

She lifted her head, breathed in and said, 'You don't believe me, do you?'

'Of *course* I do,' he said, trying to sound reassuring.

She relaxed a little. 'I thought you were . . . I thought you might be just pacifying me.'

He looked at her strangely. 'Oh no, sweetheart. If you think you saw a big man in a stovepipe top hat coming after you, then I believe you.'

She frowned. 'But Paul, I *did* see a big man in a stovepipe top hat.'

'And I *believe* you. Now exactly what did he look like? How big was he?'

'Very big. That's not the same as saying that you agree that there was a man out there.'

'Well, I don't know *what* you actually saw, do I? I have to rely on what you tell me.'

Helen considered pursuing the matter, then decided against it and said, 'Don't be long, sweetheart. Tea will only be a few minutes.'

It was 8.28 a.m., Wednesday, 13 November 2013. Angel was in his office going through the post when there was a knock at the door.

'Come in,' he called.

It was Ahmed. He had a sheet of A4 in his hand. 'Good morning, sir.'

Angel had his head in the *Police Gazette*. He was looking to see if there was anybody in there he knew.

Ahmed said, 'That man you were looking for, sir, Viktor Berezin.'

Angel promptly looked up. 'What, lad? What about Viktor Berezin?'

'He's a TV producer, sir. He seems to specialize in game-show-type programmes.'

'What do you mean, lad?' Angel said.

'Well, shows like *One, Two, Three, Go*, *Never on A Sunday*, *Two for A Pair* and *Wanna Be Rich?*. My mother loves *Wanna Be Rich?*. She watches it every Sunday evening. She loves that man on it, Alan de Souza.'

Angel's face brightened. 'Well done, Ahmed. Where's Berezin live?'

'I don't know that, sir. But I can ring the studio.'

There was a knock at the door. It opened. It was Trevor Crisp.

'Come in, lad,' he said, then he turned back to Ahmed and said, 'That's great stuff, Ahmed. Do that, ASAP. And keep me posted. I have some important questions to put to that man.'

Ahmed went out and closed the door.

Angel looked up at Crisp. 'Ah, now, lad, you went to look up Jeni Lowe's original address, didn't you?' he said. He pointed at the chair opposite him. 'Tell me, who lives there?'

'Mr and Mrs Lowe, her parents, in their early fifties.'

'Did they know what had happened to Jeni?'

'No, sir. I had to tell them.'

Angel pursed his lips. It was an awful job but it had to be done. 'Did Jeni Lowe have any brothers or sisters?'

'Two sisters. Both away from home working as cabin crew on airlines.'

'Very nice. Had Jeni ever had her life threatened, as far as they knew?'

'No, sir. They were astounded when I told them that the braking system on her car had been interfered with. They couldn't imagine who would do that to her.'

'Did you ask them if they had any idea where she might have been earlier that Sunday evening?'

'They had no inkling of what she got up to. She said that she had a happy social life in Bromersley and left it at that. She didn't want to talk about it — not with them, anyway.'

'Did they say anything about her character, her personality, her ability and so on?'

'They said that she was a natural academic.'

'She was as thick as Strangeways' gravy?' Angel asked.

Crisp shrugged. 'That's not what *they* said, sir.'

'What else did they say?'

'That she was a very hard worker, and was gifted with a vivid imagination and fanciful ideas.'

'When was the last time they saw her?'

'She went back to them most weekends. She was home the weekend of the 2nd and 3rd November but not last weekend.'

'Hmm. Did the Lowes know anything about Jeni's relationships?'

'Not recently. She didn't volunteer any information about boyfriends to them, and they'd stopped asking.'

'Hmm. That's too bad.' Angel wrinkled up his nose. 'Hmm. That's another dead end,' he said. 'Anyway, we can record them as next of kin, and one or both of them should formally identify her. Will you see to that, lad?'

The phone rang. Angel reached out for it.

'Martin Edwards here, sir. We've finished examining Jeni Lowe's car.'

'Yes, Martin, and what have you found?'

'There are good, clear prints inside around the nearside front seat, sir, which are *not* hers. Then we've found prints on the front offside door handle, the window, the steering wheel and gear stick, which *are* hers. It looks like a mostly one-person car, which has had a passenger only on rare occasions.'

'Right, Martin. Check those prints with records, and let me have the results ASAP. Anything else?'

'Well, sir, I'm not sure if it's important but we've found a small plastic cap or top or cover of something in a dull blue plastic. It was under the seat on the nearside front. No clear prints on it. Are you interested in it?'

'I don't know. I'd better have a look at it. Could have been left by the murderer, I suppose. Send it across.'

'Right, sir.'

Angel replaced the phone.

He had hardly started on his notes when there was a knock at the door. It was Ahmed, smiling from ear to ear. 'That Viktor Berezin you are looking for, sir,' he said. 'I've found him. He lives at Malibu Beach.'

Angel blinked.

'Yes, sir,' Ahmed said, referring to his notebook. '10660 Westward Boulevard, Malibu Beach, California 90267, USA.'

With a straight face, Angel said, 'Well, I can't go over there before lunch.'

'No, sir,' Ahmed said with a smile. 'But Mr Berezin will be at Zenith Television until after Christmas. One of his shows, *Wanna Be Rich?*, is being broadcast live from there until the end of January. It is not known what his plans are after that. He has many TV interests on a worldwide basis.'

'Where have you got all this stuff from, Ahmed?'

'The publicity department at Zenith Studios, sir. The woman there said he has an office there.'

'Good. Make me an appointment to see him, will you?'

'Right, sir.'

Ahmed opened the door and found DS Taylor just arriving.

Angel saw him. 'What is it, Don?' he said.

'That bottle you found in the brambles near the victim, sir,' Taylor said. 'It *had* contained whisky . . . there's a full set of digits of the right hand clear enough. I've put them through records and they have no match.'

The corners of Angel's mouth turned downwards. 'And they don't belong to the dead girl?'

'No, sir.'

'You agree that the bottle had not been there long?'

'I do, sir.'

'So it is very likely something to do with the case?'

'Very likely, sir.'

'That's what I think. But what?' There was silence for a few seconds, then Angel said, 'Right, Don, thank you.'

Taylor went out.

Angel reached for the phone. He tapped in the number of the mortuary at Bromersley General Hospital and was soon speaking to his old friend.

'Can you tell me any more about Jeni Lowe, Mac?'

'You'll be getting my full PM report by email tomorrow, Michael. Can you not wait until then?'

'As a matter of fact, Mac, I'm stuck. There's no info. So little to go on. Can you tell me, for instance, if she was stone cold sober at the time of the accident?'

'It's hard to be absolute about that, Michael, but neither drugs nor alcohol were indicated in her blood stream. And her kidneys were very healthy, which suggests she had not been a serious drinker either.'

'So it's reasonable to assume that the accident and therefore her death are entirely a result of the deliberate interference with the brakes on her car.'

'Aye, I would certainly say that, Michael.'

'And was the girl pregnant?'

'No, she wasn't, and as far as I could see, physically she was a perfectly healthy young woman of around twenty-six years of age. No tattoos and no body piercing. She might have lived to be a hundred if she hadn't hit a tree in a runaway car.'

There was a knock at the door. 'Excuse me, Mac,' he said.

He covered the mouthpiece and called, 'Come in.'

It was Ahmed.

'What is it, lad?'

'A constable has just brought this round, sir,' he said. He held out a small polythene bag which contained a blue plastic cover or stopper. 'DS Edwards from the station garage sent it, sir.'

Angel's eyebrows went up. He took the little bag from him and eyed it eagerly. 'If it wasn't a possession of Jeni Lowe's, it must have been left by the murderer. Have you any idea what it is?'

'The top or cover of something, sir?'

Angel shrugged. He knew that. 'All right, lad. Thank you.'

Returning to the phone, Angel said, 'Sorry about that, Mac.' He then went on to describe the blue plastic part and asked the pathologist for any suggestions as to what it might be.

'How big is it, Michael?'

Angel took a ruler out of his top drawer and measured it.

'It's roughly an inch by half an inch by just over half an inch. And it's sort of lozenge shaped.'

'Has it got any screw threads on it?'

'No. But it has ridges inside the rim, so it could presumably be snapped on to something.'

'It's not off a scent bottle then,' Mac said. 'It's probably no more than a piece off a bairn's toy.'

'You might be right, Mac. But at the moment, it's *all* I've got.'

'Good luck, Michael.'

Angel replaced the phone.

He had never relied on luck in the past and now wasn't the time to start. He took out an envelope on which he kept his notes. He went down them systematically to see what avenue he might explore next. It would have been useful to find out where Jeni Lowe had been earlier that Sunday evening. Her mobile phone was missing. It would have been a big help in illustrating who she was in touch with, and where she might have been shortly before the fatal crash. He had asked her workmates and they had no ideas, and her parents weren't able to throw any light on the situation either.

He was still thinking about that when there was a knock on the door. It was Ahmed.

'I've got an appointment at Zenith Television Studios for you, sir,' he said, 'to see Mr Berezin at ten o'clock tomorrow morning. I hope that's convenient. The woman said you won't be allowed very long.'

'That's great, Ahmed, thank you. I hope you told her it was police business and not an out-of-work actor looking for a job.'

'I did, sir.'

Suddenly there was a strange tinny, whirring sound.

Angel looked up. 'What's that?'

'Oh,' Ahmed said. 'That's my new watch, sir.' He pulled up his jacket sleeve proudly and showed Angel the bright gold wristwatch.

'What's that noise?'

'The alarm, sir,' he said, switching it off. 'Sorry about that. I haven't got used to it yet. It's a copy of the £12,000 Swiss Mitto-Amino watch.'

Angel frowned. He tried to look interested.

Ahmed said, 'As well as London, it tells the time in New York, Sydney and Tokyo.'

'Well, what's the time *now*?' Angel said, looking at the dial. 'It says 3.17. That's not right. It's nearly twelve o'clock.'

'No. I haven't set it right yet, sir. It takes some getting used to. It's also got a compass so that you know in what direction you're travelling.'

'Where did you get that from?'

'A neighbour. It was an unwanted gift. He had it given and he already had one. He let me have it cheap.'

'I should get it set to the right time.'

The phone rang. Angel reached out for it.

'I will, sir. I will,' Ahmed said, scrutinizing the dial on his way to the door.

'Angel,' he said into the phone, watching Ahmed shake his wrist violently several times then peer again at the dial.

It was the station civilian telephone receptionist. 'There's a man whose name is Abercrombie of The Bailiff's House, Long Lane. He says you know him. He's very anxious to speak to you—'

'Put him through, miss.'

'Oh? Right,' she said. 'You're through, Inspector.'

Angel said, 'Hello. Is that Mr Abercrombie?'

'Ah, there you are, young fellow my lad. Inspector Angel. Just the one. Now see here, I'm in a spot of bother, old chap, and I want you to come down here so that we can talk about it, sort of thing. Very important.'

Angel rubbed his chin. 'Well, Mr Abercrombie, is it to do with the young woman neighbour of yours who died in the car crash?'

'Oh yes, old chap. The very thing. Oh, do hurry up. Get it off my chest, don't you know. Man to man.'

Angel frowned. It sounded as if he wanted to confess something. 'Is it anything we can discuss on the phone?' he said.

'Oh, do come down here, old chap. Can't get to *you*, else I would. Osteoarthritis. Something you would want to know.

The hips, you know. Soon as you can. The weather, damned wicked. Quid pro quo. Information. I know something — well, I *might* know something — and I've not been exactly straight up, don't you know? Quid pro quo. That's what I want. A special arrangement with you. Look, time's running out.'

'I'll come straightaway.'

'Good chap. You won't regret it.'

Angel replaced the phone and pursed his lips. He felt as if a wild bird was inside his chest, flapping its wings, and a big bass drum was banging out a fast beat. At last! A possible new line of inquiry.

He reached into his drawer for his buttonhole recorder. He checked the state of the battery, slipped the slim recorder into his inside jacket pocket and threaded the wire from it through a small hole he had made behind the lapel, then he fastened the mike with adhesive tape to the suit material. He pushed the swivel chair back, stood up, and was putting one arm in the sleeve of his overcoat as the phone rang.

He looked at it, pulled a disagreeable face, hesitated, put his arm in the other sleeve then reached out for it.

'Angel,' he said into the mouthpiece.

It was his boss, Superintendent Horace Harker, who coughed several times, cleared his throat and then said, 'Ah, Angel. Come up here. Something urgent has cropped up.'

Angel sighed. 'I was just on my way out, sir,' he said. 'I have an important call to see a witness in this Jeni Lowe murder case. Can I call in on my way back?'

'No, that will keep,' he said. 'This is urgent. Come up here straightaway.' There was a loud click in the earpiece as Harker banged down the phone.

Angel's fists tightened as he stormed up the corridor. He soon arrived outside a door with 'Superintendent H. Harker' painted on it. He sighed, knocked on the door, pushed it open and went in. An invisible curtain of hot air reeking of menthol hit him in the face. It was accompanied by the sound of the gentle whirring of two portable electric fan heaters directed towards Harker's feet.

The superintendent was a thin man with a turnip-shaped head, very little hair, and a ginger and grey moustache. He had a small mouth and big ears. Angel often thought his head looked like a skull with ears attached.

As Angel entered, Harker looked up from behind three separate piles of files, letters, reports, boxes of tissues and Movicol on his desk.

'Come in, Angel,' he said. He pointed to a chair opposite him. 'This Viktor Berezin . . . you mentioned him in your report. Tell me about him.'

Angel licked his bottom lip with the tip of his tongue. 'Could we not do this later, sir? I have a witness who seems to be anxious to tell me something urgently. It would be a pity—'

'No. This is important, Angel. Tell me about this Viktor Berezin.'

Angel sighed and sat down in the chair opposite. 'Well, sir, I found his name in Jeni Lowe's notebook. That's all. We have tracked him down. Apparently he is a television producer and I have an appointment—'

Harker's eyes suddenly shone angrily. *'Television?'*

'Yes, sir. And I have an appointment to see him at the studios in Leeds tomorrow.'

'Oh, I see,' Harker said with a sniff. 'So you're now planning a career on the small screen, are you?'

Angel frowned. 'No, sir.'

'You're going to have them make a star out of you, are you? Not content with appearing in the papers as the detective who *always gets his man*, you now want to be on television. Are they going to make a series out of you? Well, you're scruffy enough to play Columbo, I suppose.'

'No,' Angel said. 'It's nothing like that at all. It's a simple, straightforward interview of a witness. That's all.'

'It had better be. What concerns me is that that man, Viktor Berezin, is a Russian, isn't he?'

'Don't know, sir.'

'Well, I don't want you meddling around with a powerful Russian oligarch, if that's what he is. They're very secretive and difficult to deal with. They are like the Chinese, you can't tell what they're thinking. We'd be safer bringing in Special Branch. They're trained and equipped for dealing with such characters.'

'I hardly think he is a Russian oligarch, sir. His address is in the States and he is the producer of television games such as *Wanna Be Rich?*.'

Harker pursed his lips and frowned. Eventually he said, 'Oh, I see. Well, I hope you're right.'

Angel also hoped he was right.

Harker suddenly looked up and said, 'Well, cut along then, lad. I thought you had a witness to see urgently.'

Angel's face went scarlet. The muscles round his mouth and jaw tightened. He pushed himself out of the chair towards the door. 'Yes, sir,' he said.

He banged Harker's office door, ran down the corridor, then turned left past the cells, through the rear door and outside to his car.

FIVE

It was 1 p.m. exactly when Angel pulled the BMW into the side of the narrow lane outside The Bailiff's House and turned off the ignition.

He got out of the car and looked round. A thin stream of smoke emerged from the chimney. Everywhere was quiet; unusually quiet. He locked the car and went up the path to the back of the house.

He put his hand up to knock at the door but stopped when he noticed it was ajar. He gave it a gentle push and it swung open to reveal the small kitchen-cum-dining-room floor, table and other furniture littered with papers, magazines, letters, cutlery, pans and other cooking implements. He looked up and saw a pale white patch on the wallpaper over the fireplace where he remembered a painting of a hunting scene had been. His heart began to beat faster as he realized that old man Abercrombie had had unwelcome visitors. And they couldn't have been long gone.

He stepped into the room and saw and felt the warmth of the open fire. He looked round at the untidy mess. Then in the corner of the room between built-in cupboards and an easy chair, he saw the crumpled figure of Mr Abercrombie.

His face and head were bloody, his eyes were closed. He was motionless.

Angel's pulse banged faster and harder until he could hear it drumming in his ears. He dashed across to him and kneeled down by his side. He put his fingertips on his neck. He was still warm. There was a slight pulse. Angel's heart rose. He dived into his pocket, took out his mobile, tapped in 999 and asked for an ambulance.

As he closed the phone, Abercrombie opened one eye, then the other. He immediately began to shake.

Angel said, 'It's all right, Mr Abercrombie, it's Michael Angel. Who did this to you?'

Abercrombie looked into Angel's face; it took several seconds for him to stop shaking and focus his eyes. He sighed, then smiled.

Angel reached for his hand and gently squeezed it. 'You're going to be all right. I've sent for an ambulance.'

'Angel, old chap, don't bother. Look, before I go, I must tell you something.'

Angel remembered he had set up his buttonhole recorder. He reached into his inside pocket and switched it on.

Then he said, 'Who did this to you? What happened?'

Abercrombie began. It was a great struggle for him to speak. 'It was me who . . .' His voice trailed away.

Angel rubbed his hand and said, 'Come on, Mr Abercrombie, tell me who did this to you.'

'I was up there looking for kindling. Keep the fire going. I opened the car door . . . helped the girl out of the damned thing before it . . . anyway she told me about the racket and that I should tell the police about him . . . but I thought that . . .' His voice trailed away again. His eyes closed.

Angel muscles tightened. He reached out to both his hands and gently squeezed them. 'Come on, Mr Abercrombie. Tell me who did this to you.'

Abercrombie opened his eyes again. His chest was heaving.

Angel looked into his face. It was a mass of wounds and congealed blood.

‘Who did this to you?’ Angel said. ‘Tell me, Mr Abercrombie, *please.*’

Abercrombie breathed unevenly several times and then, taking a deep breath, he said, ‘I took the girl’s money and watch and ring and phone. May I be forgiven? Tried to get money out of *him* too . . . not a bean, old chap . . . he’s a monster . . . he’s found a money tree . . .’

At that point, Abercrombie’s eyes closed, his head dropped forward and his chest stopped heaving.

Angel reached out for the old man’s hands again but there was no response. He touched his neck. There was no pulse.

Angel gently lowered Abercrombie’s head and shoulders back down on to the stone floor, stood up, looked into the yellow flames of the fire and sighed.

It was three minutes to ten the next day, Thursday, when Angel walked up to the reception desk at Zenith Television in Leeds. ‘I am Detective Inspector Angel,’ he said to the young lady behind the desk. ‘I’ve an appointment with Mr Berezin at ten o’clock.’

‘Would you kindly take a seat while I locate Mr Berezin for you?’ she said.

Angel looked round the reception area at the white painted walls adorned with forty or fifty blown-up portraits of current famous faces in the entertainment business. He was thinking how few he could name.

A lift door opened and a noisy group of young women spilled out. In the middle of them was a man in his thirties in a very well-cut light grey suit. He was suntanned and looked as if he had just walked out of a Savile Row tailor’s window. The young women were screeching and screaming for his attention and brushing as close to him as they could as he walked along. He merely glanced at them from time to time, unsmilingly, as he made his way to the reception desk.

The man said something to the receptionist, who pointed to Angel. He then nodded and crossed over to him. The throng of females accompanied him.

'I am Viktor Berezin,' he announced. He had a deep voice and spoke with a slight East European accent. 'You vanted to see me?'

'Yes, sir,' Angel said.

The women then looked at Angel. They turned to each other with quizzical looks, saying, 'Who is he?' 'Don't know.' 'Do you recognize him?' 'No.'

One girl turned to him and said, 'Are you anybody, sir?'

Angel smiled at the question. 'No,' he said, 'Afraid not.'

Meanwhile to whoops of delight, Berezin was signing the young ladies autograph books. He rattled through them very quickly. Some thanked him, some kissed him on the cheeks or the forehead, much to his feigned protestations. Then they all filtered away, looking round for someone else to buttonhole.

Berezin then turned to Angel and said, 'It is the same everyvere I go. Nossing I can do about it. Now, you are from ze police, are you not?'

'Bromersley force,' Angel said.

'Please follow me.'

He directed Angel into a small empty room with four chairs and a small desk.

There was a card hanging on the knob of the door on the inside. It read *INTERVIEW IN PROGRESS*. Berezin hung it on the outside doorknob.

'There,' Berezin said. 'We shall not be interrupted, Inspector. Now what is it that the English police could possibly want from me?'

Angel quickly explained the circumstances of the murder of Jeni Lowe and how he had found Berezin's name written in a particular way on her notebook. Then he showed him the photograph of her in her passport.

Berezin frowned. 'Yes, I do remember ze young lady's face. Very pretty.'

'How close did you get to her, Mr Berezin? Did you meet her somewhere? Did you take her out on a date?'

'No. No. I would certainly have remembered if I had had such a close relationship as that. Tell me, Inspector Angel, was she a contestant or an actress or somesing?'

'No. She worked in advertising,' Angel said, 'And while you think about that, Mr Berezin, can you tell me where you were last Sunday night?'

'Sunday night? That was the night they were broadcasting *Wanna Be Rich?*. I was in my hotel suite watching the show, of course.'

'Which hotel was that?' Angel said.

'The MacNaughton on the Headrow, here in Leeds.'

'Who were you with?'

'I vas on my own.'

'Can anybody vouch for you? Did you have any contact with any member of the hotel staff, for instance?'

Berezin frowned. 'I don't sink so.'

Angel shook his head.

Berezin said, 'She worked in advertising, you said? Which company did she work for?'

'The Meyer Agency.'

'Ze Meyer Agency. Oh yes. I remember now. She was present at meetings — several meetings — we had a few months ago regarding the presentation proposals to market the format of the show of *Wanna Be Rich?* at the Rome Film Festival.'

Angel's face brightened. 'How well did you get to know her?'

'I didn't,' he said bluntly. 'She answered my questions. That's all, really.'

'Who else was at the meetings?'

'There were just the two from Meyer. Their creative director — I forget his name — and the girl, and supporting me were Alan de Souza, and Dennis Grant. They are the presenter and director here, in the UK.'

Angel pursed his lips. 'And how many meetings where Jeni Lowe was present were there?'

'Three or four, I suppose.'

'Don't you know?'

'Inspector, I attend meetings all day long. My life is made up of meetings. That's how I run my business. De Souza or Grant would be able to tell you that accurately if it matters so much.'

'Did Jeni Lowe meet anybody else besides de Souza and Grant?'

'I don't know.'

'How friendly were these meetings? Did you or any of them pair off and have a meal together, for example?'

'Probably, possibly. I don't believe I did, but I cannot speak for any of the others. But what you are most interested in is the young lady, Jeni Lowe, isn't it? And I can tell you that I didn't have any contact with her outside ze meeting rooms. Believe me, Inspector, I have a surfeit of women in my life. I do not need another.'

Angel looked at him, nodded and rubbed his chin. 'Very well, Mr Berezin, how can I make contact with de Souza and Grant?'

'They are both in the building, Inspector. Would you like me to see if I can reach one or both of them?'

'Thank you,' Angel said.

Berezin reached out for the phone on the desk and tapped in a number.

Angel pushed his notebook back into his pocket. As he did so his fingers touched the plastic top or cap that had been found in Jeni Lowe's car. He took it out.

Berezin muttered something into the phone. 'I have asked a runner to find them and ask them to ring this number. It won't take long, I am sure.' He stood up.

Angel then held up the blue plastic top or cap. 'Can you tell me what this is from?'

Berezin took it, looked at it carefully then handed it back. 'I'm afraid not. Is it from a Christmas cracker?'

Angel shrugged. 'Don't know. I hope to find out.'

The phone rang. Berezin answered it. ''Allo? . . . Yes . . . Come up to ze interview room at reception straightavay.'

He replaced the phone and turned to Angel. 'That's Alan de Souza, the presenter. You may have heard of him. He's a bit . . . er brash, but he's all right.'

'Thank you,' Angel said.

'I must get on, Inspector,' he said, reaching out for the door handle. 'You will excuse me, please?'

'Of course.'

The phone rang again. Berezin turned back and answered it. The conversation with the caller was very brief. It took only a few seconds, then he replaced the phone, turned to Angel and said, 'Zat was Dennis Grant. He's the director of the show. I told him you wanted to see him here in ten minutes. I trust that is OK.'

Angel smiled. 'Thank you again.'

'I hope you find ze girl's murderer.'

Angel nodded. They shook hands and he was gone.

Angel took the opportunity to bring his notes up to date.

Several minutes later, Alan de Souza came in.

'Inspector Angel?' he said. 'You wanted to see me?'

'Yes. Come in. Please sit down.'

'I hope this won't take long. I need to be at a rehearsal in a few minutes.'

'I hope not.'

Angel quickly explained that he was making inquiries into the death of Jeni Lowe and asked him if he knew her.

'I don't believe I've heard of her,' he said.

Angel showed him her passport photograph.

De Souza shook his head. 'I meet hundreds of girls and young women in television. This business is, sadly, littered with them . . . hundreds of them . . . chasing after sex or fame or both. I can't be expected to remember everyone I meet.'

Angel nodded. 'She worked for The Meyer Agency. Does that refresh your memory?'

He frowned. 'Oh yes. Indeed it does. She was a copywriter with a smooth account executive pitching a presentation about marketing the format of our show abroad.'

'And what did you think of her?'

'You'd have to give me notice of a question like that, Inspector. I only saw her for a few minutes. I don't think we even spoke to each other. She seemed a presentable young woman. She didn't have any special features like a big nose, a tattoo on her arm or any metalwork hanging off her face. And I believe, from memory, she wore a conventional skirt and top.'

'Yes, Mr de Souza, but did you *like* her?'

'I didn't get to know her, Inspector. She was here to sell Berezin a marketing scheme. I was only brought in with Dennis Grant to give our opinion.'

'I take it you didn't like her?'

'Not much, no. I do hate it when women bring sex into marketing.'

'So, obviously you never saw her . . . socially, out of the office, after work?'

'Of course not.'

Angel said, 'Do you happen to know if she paired off with anybody else? If anybody else had a meal with her, took her out or developed any sort of a relationship with her?'

De Souza shrugged. 'No, I can't say that I saw her with anybody outside the meetings, Inspector, but it happens all the time. Women have always been the cause of men's downfall, haven't they? Dennis Grant might possibly be able to tell you more. You're seeing him next, I believe. He's almost as popular with the girls as Viktor Berezin.'

Angel rubbed his chin. De Souza seemed to have covered the point. He moved on.

'Where were you last Sunday evening?' Angel asked.

He held out his arms and hands palm upwards and said, 'I was here, presenting the show, wasn't I?'

Angel nodded, then he reached into his pocket and took out the blue plastic cap or top. He held it up between finger and thumb and said, 'Do you know what this is?'

De Souza took it, turned it over in his hand then passed it back. 'Sorry. No idea. Was it found on the body?'

'No,' Angel said, then he added, 'Well, Mr de Souza, thank you very much, that's all for now.'

'Ah, good,' de Souza said. Then he stood up, crossed the room to the door, opened it, glanced at his watch and looked back at Angel. 'I'll just about make the rehearsal, thank you,' he said. 'Goodbye, nice to have met you, Inspector.'

'Goodbye, Mr de Souza,' Angel said.

Then he went out, leaving the door open.

Angel noticed a tall man standing there, smiling.

Angel blinked and said, 'Mr Grant?'

'And you must be the famous Inspector Angel, from Bromersley police if my memory serves me right — the policeman who always gets his man, like the proverbial Mountie.'

'I suppose I am,' Angel said, standing back to let him in.

Grant continued: 'I was reading about you the other day in a magazine at the dentist's. It was about the murder outside a scrapyard of a man in his bare feet. Then you discovered that the murderer was also in bare feet. It seemed a most convoluted and difficult case of murder. Anyway, you sorted it all out. You exposed the murderer and he got life.'

Angel wished he wouldn't go on about what he had read about him. He closed the door and pointed at a chair. 'Please sit down, Mr Grant.'

'I understand from Viktor that this is about a young lady from The Meyer Agency, Jeni something or other. Well, Inspector, I can tell you that I know very little about her. She was at several presentation meetings about promoting the format of *Wanna Be Rich?* abroad earlier this year. That's all I know.'

'You never went out with her, or met her outside those meetings?'

'No. And I never saw anybody else show any particular interest in her either. She was such a pretty young thing. I can't understand why anybody would want to kill her, I really can't.'

'Nor can I,' Angel said. Then he said, 'Where were you on Sunday afternoon and evening?'

‘I was in the studio most of that time. We rehearse the show from around noon until five o’clock. Then we are supposed to rest . . . until we assemble to transmit the show live at 8.30.’

‘Where were you between five and 8.30?’

‘Well, I can’t really leave the building. Most of the time I was in my office, being on hand for what last-minute changes or emergencies might crop up. I might nip into the canteen for a cup of tea, or down to the studio to check on something. I’m never far away.’

Angel nodded. He fumbled around in his jacket pocket and took out the blue plastic top or cap that he had found in Jeni Lowe’s car.

‘Have you any idea what this is?’ he said.

Grant took it. He frowned and turned it over in his hand. His eyebrows went up. ‘Is it the top of a computer memory stick?’ he said.

Angel’s jaw dropped. He thought a moment and rapidly sucked in a mouthful of air. He could be right. He took it back from the man and had another close look at it. It was the same shape and general design, but was about double the size. He relaxed and exhaled. ‘No. It’s too big. But thank you.’

‘Pleasure,’ Grant said.

Angel pocketed the bit of plastic. He got up. He thought he had asked him all the relevant questions for the moment so he shook Grant’s hand and took his leave.

SIX

Angel arrived back at his office at about twelve noon. He picked up the phone and summoned Ahmed. The young man arrived with his notebook.

'Ahmed,' Angel said, 'I want you to run a check on these three men: Viktor Berezin, Dennis Grant and Alan de Souza.'

'Right, sir.'

'And are there any messages from DS Taylor or Dr Mac?'

'No, sir.'

Angel rubbed his chin.

Suddenly there was a dull whirring sound.

'What's that?' he said.

'Sorry, sir,' Ahmed said, looking at his wrist. 'It's the alarm on my watch again. I mustn't have set it right.'

Ahmed pressed a button on the side of the watch and the alarm stopped.

Angel said, 'Does that watch tell you the right time now?'

'Well, yes sir,' he said. 'It's set at the right time for Tokyo.'

'But we're *not* in Tokyo.'

'Well, I seem to have pressed the wrong button.'

'Aren't there any instructions with it?'

'Yes, sir.'

'Well, follow the instructions then.'

'They're in Norwegian, sir. We didn't do that at school. Do you speak Norwegian, sir?'

Angel blinked. He rubbed his chin very hard. The question was trying his patience. 'I should take it back to the man you bought it off, lad.'

'Can't do that, sir. He's our next-door neighbour. He was doing me a *big* favour. It came in its original box and it only cost me £100.'

'It's £100 too much for a watch if it doesn't tell you the time.'

'I'll get the hang of it, sir.'

He went out.

Angel reached for the phone. He wanted to speak to DS Taylor.

'What have you got, Don?'

'Well, sir, there's quite a lot of blood splashes in Abercrombie's front room as well as in the kitchen, indicating that Abercrombie put up quite a struggle with his assailant. The first blow was probably delivered in the front room and apparently continued in the kitchen, so in spite of his age and frailty, he was no pushover.'

Angel thought he must have been a very courageous man. 'Have you any idea what weapon was used?'

'No, sir.'

'Have you come across anything there that might have belonged to Jeni Lowe?'

'No, sir. Nothing feminine at all. Very much a bachelor's pad — if you know what I mean?'

'Right, Don. Let me know when you have completed the sweep and I'll come straight down.'

'We'll be through in about twenty minutes, sir.'

'Right,' he said.

He promptly cancelled the call and tapped in the number for the mortuary at Bromersley General Hospital.

He was soon speaking to Dr Mac.

'Old man Abercrombie took quite a beating, Michael,' Mac said. 'When we got his clothes off, there were contusions on his neck, shoulders, arms and head commensurate with blows made with a rigid bar or rod of some kind, probably made from iron or steel . . . could have been a heavy poker, for instance.'

'I'll have a look when I get to the scene. Anything else?'

'Aye. A few threads of hair from the front of Abercrombie's waistcoat and one from the back of his hand will be from his assailant. It looks as if Abercrombie held the assailant by his hair at some point in the attack.'

Angel had nothing but admiration for the old man, who would have been fighting for his life. 'It sounds very likely, Mac,' he said. 'And the DNA from the hairs will be very welcome to prove the case, if and when I get a suspect. The murderer had been very careful not to leave any clue when he interfered with the brakes causing the death of Jeni Lowe. He has not been quite so clever in his assault and murder of old Mr Abercrombie.'

It was Friday, 15 November. The rain had stopped and the winds had eased a little.

Cora Blenkinsop opened the back door of The Brambles and poured a bucket of dirty water down the outside grate. She closed the door, put the bucket and mop in the pantry, looked round the kitchen to see that everything was tidy, checked the time on the kitchen clock, then went into the hall to the bottom of the stairs.

'Mrs Rose!' she called, while pulling on her overcoat. 'I've finished the kitchen. And it's half past twelve.'

'All right, Cora,' Helen Rose said. 'I'm ready.' She appeared at the head of the stairs and began to descend. 'You're sure I'm not putting you out of your way?'

'Nah,' she said. 'It's nobbut a cockstride. And it'll only take a minute.'

Helen Rose checked that the front door was locked and they left by the back door, which she also locked and checked. They walked down the short path to the side gate and they were out on to Havercroft Lane. It was a five-minute walk to the main Bromersley to Sheffield Road, which was only a mile from Bromersley town centre. They were now in a built-up area with houses on each side of the road and an Anglican church, St Thomas's, on the right about 200 yards down.

'That's the church, Mrs Rose,' Cora said.

Helen Rose followed Cora Blenkinsop through the iron gate into the churchyard. They passed the main door of the church and went straight down the path along the side of it to where most of the gravestones were to be found.

'I seem to remember that it's a double one, next to the path on the right,' Cora Blenkinsop said as she began to check the names on the gravestones.

Helen Rose followed behind. She looked round to see if anybody was watching them. Several crows croaked something unwelcoming. Her hands were cold, but so was her back and her legs. She was shivering. She really didn't want to be checking up on the miserable history of the people who had previously lived in her house, and she wished she was somewhere else.

'Ah,' Cora said. 'This is it, Mrs Rose.' She began to read. '*Here lies the body of Elsie Cudlipp . . .*'

Helen Rose rushed up to her side. She looked at the large stone at the head of a double-spaced grave. She continued with the reading, a few words at a time, in a quiet quavering voice:

'*Here lies the body of Elsie Cudlipp, who died on February 15, 1741, in the thirtieth year of her age. Also her son, Rupert Cudlipp, who died in the twelfth year of his age. Also her daughter, Nancy Cudlipp, who died in the eleventh year of her age. Also her maid, Clarice Evangeline Morpeth, who died in the fourteenth year of her age. May God grant them the peace they never had in their lifetime. RIP.*'

'I told you it was there,' Cora said.

'Yes . . . It's too awful to think about,' Helen Rose said.

'And I told you Amos Cudlipp *wasn't* there cos he's in your garden somewhere. He couldn't be buried in constipated ground.'

It was two o'clock when Angel arrived outside The Bailiff's House, parking the BMW well into the side of the narrow lane. The sky was full of black clouds. The wind was blowing noisily and it was much colder. It seemed cold enough for snow. He went through the gate, up the path to the back door. He banged on the door and a member of the SOCO team donned in the sterile disposable white paper overalls let him in.

'Thank you, lad. Where's DS Taylor?'

'I'm here, sir,' Taylor said, coming through the door that led to the rest of the house. He was also dressed in a sterile overall. He pulled down the mask from over his mouth and said, 'We've finished the sweep.'

'Good,' Angel said. 'Dr Mac said that the murder weapon was an iron or steel bar . . .'

'Is this it?' Taylor said, pointing to a heavy iron poker about a yard long, made from half-inch-square extruded iron, twisted to create a design and with a piece of a larger diameter welded to it to form a handle. It was on the floor under the table.

'Any prints anywhere?'

'The handle has been wiped clean, sir. But there is blood and several grey hairs on the other end.'

Angel's face muscles tightened. 'Vicious-looking weapon,' he said. 'Right. Let Mac see it. Then let me have it. It will have to be entered as an exhibit.'

Taylor nodded. 'Right, sir.'

'Found anything feminine in the place? Anything that could have belonged to Jeni Lowe?'

'No, sir. And we've looked everywhere. He seems to be a man who has never been interested in the fair sex. Cricket and horse-racing seem to have been his main interests.'

'I was hoping that there would be some evidence to confirm the story he confessed to me that he took Jeni Lowe's money, watch, ring and phone.'

Taylor shook his head. 'Nothing of that sort here, sir,' he said. 'Unless it is very well hidden.'

'Unless it is *very* well hidden,' Angel repeated slowly while rubbing his chin. After a few moments he said, 'I wonder.'

Taylor frowned. 'What's that, sir?'

'I was thinking,' he said, 'if Jeni Lowe left her mobile switched on, and if I dialled her number . . .'

He reached into his inside pocket and took out the scrap of paper with her number on that was given to him at the advertising agency. Then he took out his own mobile and tapped the number into it. He didn't expect a reply but he certainly hoped he might hear it ring. He pressed the send button and after a second or two they heard a phone connect and ring out.

Angel's eyes met Taylor's. They thought it was in the other downstairs room, the sitting room. There were two SOCO men working in there: one had a camera and the other was holding a shaded electric lamp to provide a light source.

The ringing was coming from a wall, against which was a settee.

Angel said, 'Excuse us, lads. We're trying to locate that phone.'

'It's under the settee, sir,' one of them said.

'Move it, will you? We've got to trace it before the battery runs out.'

Angel, Taylor and the other SOCO men dragged the settee away from the wall.

The phone was still ringing out but weakly.

Taylor said, 'It's coming from somewhere under the carpet.'

Angel peeled back the carpet and the underlay. He tapped around looking for a loose floorboard or two. Then he saw two short pieces. They were also loose. He knew he was not far away. He lifted them up easily and the volume of the ring increased appreciably. Underneath, between the joists, he saw a white plastic shopping bag with the word Tesco plastered across it in red. He lifted it out.

'Bingo!' he said. Then he looked inside the cavity to see if anything else was there. There was nothing but hundred-year-old wood shavings and dust. He stood up.

'Thank you for your help, lads,' he said.

'That's all right, sir.'

'Take a pic of that hiding place then put it back together, will you?' he said.

He went through to the kitchen where there was a bit of space on the kitchen table. Taylor followed. He opened the bag on the kitchen table and took out the contents item by item.

There was a very slim wallet containing only a bank debit card and a driver's licence, an inexpensive wristwatch, a small decorative ring of six garnets and a pearl in nine-carat gold, and a mobile phone. Angel assumed that Abercrombie had removed any cash there might have been in the wallet.

Taylor said, 'Well, sir, there isn't much there, but it shows that Abercrombie was telling the truth.'

'Yes, but I wish I knew what Jeni Lowe had told him before she died,' Angel said. 'She told him about a racket and that he should tell the police. Also Abercrombie said that he *tried* to get more out of the man — whoever he is — and that he's a monster, and that he's found a money tree.'

'Doesn't help much, sir,' Taylor said.

'No. I think Abercrombie tried to blackmail whoever it was, and the man retaliated by murdering him. I haven't seen a phone here. I assume there is one.'

'Yes, sir. It's on the floor. I assume Abercrombie pulled it off the table so that he could talk to you.'

'You don't happen to know the number, do you?'

'No, sir.'

'Right. I'll get Ahmed on to it. Let me know if anything interesting turns up here. I must get this mobile back to the office.'

Angel took his leave of Taylor, dashed out into the cold November wind, turned the BMW round and headed straight for the police station.

Ahmed saw Angel in the corridor on his way to his office through the open door of the CID office. He quickly picked up his notebook and followed the inspector into his own office.

Angel turned and saw him. 'Yes, Ahmed, what is it?'

'I've done that PNC check on Alan de Souza, Dennis Grant and Viktor Berezin, sir. And they're all "not known".'

'Oh,' Angel said and wrinkled his nose. It would have helped if one of them *had* been known. 'All right, lad. Thank you.'

'The case not going very well, sir?' Ahmed said.

Angel blew out a length of air. 'You could say that.'

'Oh. Sorry about that, sir. Is there anything I can do?'

'Aye. Two things.'

Angel put the plastic Tesco's bag on his desk, took out the mobile and handed it to him.

'This was Jeni Lowe's,' he said. 'Will you check off all the calls she made in the last two weeks?'

Ahmed smiled. 'I'll do it straightaway, sir. What was the second thing?'

'Old Mr Abercrombie's house — The Bailiff's House — has a landline. Find out the number, and check his calls for the last two weeks and let me have them ASAP.'

It was four o'clock on Friday afternoon and darkness was approaching as the November storm clouds were gathering. Helen Rose went into the small room off the hall, which she had provisionally called the study, and switched on the lights. She looked at the ancient two-bar electric fire, which had come with the house, standing in front of the stark fireplace constructed from bricks painted black. She had tried to make the little room cosy. It had two easy chairs, a desk, a swivel chair and an occasional table in the corner with a flatscreen television on it. There was a water-heated radiator on the far wall but when it was cold outside the room needed more heat and she believed that nothing was warmer than a coal fire. She made a decision. She unplugged the old fire and put it to one side.

Cora Blenkinsop was busy putting the washed pots and pans in the cupboards or on the hooks where they belonged.

'Hasn't it gone cold?' Helen Rose said.

'I reckon we'll have some snow soon.'

'Do you know how to light a coal fire?'

'I should say so, Mrs Rose. Haven't I been doing it for my mother since I was nine?'

Helen smiled. 'Will you light the fire in the study? We're going to have a proper coal fire.'

Cora stared at her. 'In the study?'

'Yes. I want it nice and warm for when my husband gets in. I'll get the coal in and bring it through.'

'But there's an electric fire in there, Mrs Rose. I don't think you're supposed to have a fire in *that* grate.'

'Why on earth not, Cora?'

'Health and safety. Something to do with the clean air laws, I think.'

'I've not heard anything about *that*.'

'Well, have you had the chimney swept recently, Mrs Rose? The smoke might come back into the house and spoil the decorations.'

Helen Rose frowned. 'If you don't want to do it, Cora, *I'll* do it.'

'No, it's not that, Mrs Rose,' she replied quickly. 'I just wouldn't want you to get into any trouble, but it's all right. If that's what you want, I'll do it straightaway.'

'Thank you, Cora,' she said and she went outside. A cold wind swirled round her. She crossed to the old slaughterhouse and opened one of the doors. She filled two buckets with coal. She carried them into the house then down to the study and put them next to Cora in the big fireplace.

Cora was making tight coils of newspaper and putting them in the grate.

Helen said nothing but she was pleased to see Cora getting on with it. She went back up to the kitchen. It was a few minutes to four, time she was getting Paul's tea ready.

Several minutes later, Cora entered the kitchen, went up to the sink, turned on the hot tap and began to wash her hands.

'Time you were off, Cora. How's that fire doing?'

'It should be drawing like mad in a few minutes,' she said as she dried her hands. 'You and Mr Rose should be as cosy as two bugs in a rug tonight,' she said with a grin.

'I hope so. Thank you very much.'

She reached out for her coat. 'See you tomorrow.'

The door slammed.

Helen Rose looked up at the clock. It said one minute past four.

It was the worst time of the day for her. She would be alone in the house until Paul arrived from work at around 5.30.

She busied herself preparing some chicken legs for a casserole.

After a few minutes, she wondered how the fire in the study was going. She wiped her hands and went down the hall to find out. As soon as she opened the door she knew it wasn't lit. There was no warmth in the air and no flame from the grate. She switched on the light. There were a few scorch marks where some of the newspaper had been burned but it clearly had not spread and had soon gone out. She went into the fireplace and kneeled down. She removed the coal pieces and the sticks and noticed that the newspaper underneath was excessively damp. In fact blobs of water had drained downward on to the tiles below.

No wonder it was not blazing.

Helen Rose frowned. It looked as if somebody had deliberately doused the fire in the grate with water.

SEVEN

It was Friday and it was 5.35 p.m.

Angel had simply had enough for another week. When he realized the time, he closed the books on his desk and pushed them and all the papers into the top drawer, reached out for his coat and went home.

It was Friday, so it was bound to be fish for tea. Poached salmon, peas and new potatoes.

He came in by the back door, gave Mary a kiss, got a beer out of the fridge and then went without a word into the sitting room. He sat down and tore the ring off the top of the can and had a swig of the beer. Then he looked round for the post.

Mary came in. 'What's the matter?' she said.

He looked up at her.

She could see from his eyes that he wasn't sure what she meant. 'Nothing,' he said. Then he added, 'I gave you a kiss, didn't I?'

'Oh yes, oh master,' Mary said, shuffling forward with her feet together and her head bowed Chinese-style. 'Most gracious of you.'

'Don't be daft,' he said. 'What's the matter with *you*?'

'I'm curious,' she said. 'I'm curious to know what's on *your* mind.'

Angel scratched his head and, lowering his eyebrows, looked at her.

'You come into the house,' she continued. 'You don't say anything. You give me a dutiful kiss across the table, get a beer and disappear into here. You treat this place as if it was a hotel.'

He frowned then said, 'What did you want me to do? Grab you by the hair, drag you upstairs and claim my conjugal rights?'

She smiled. 'No, you fool. But when you come in here with your face down to your boots, it's natural for me, as your wife, to express concern.'

'My face is not down to my boots. It's just that I'm tired and a bit fed up. And this murder case . . .'

'I knew it. I knew it would be work,' she said. 'I think it's time you gave that job up. It's getting too much for you. You take it to heart so much. Why don't you put your uniform back on and go and assist Inspector Asquith?'

'Nay, lass. Don't talk daft. For one thing it would mean a cut in money. You wouldn't like that, would you? And besides, I don't *want* to. I *like* what I do.'

'You wouldn't think so, the way you carry on.'

'Well, I've hit a brick wall, Mary. That's all. The clues are not there. I know a few bits and pieces but I am missing a big chunk of the puzzle. And I can't at the moment see a way clear to enable me to make any progress. The murderer interfered with the brakes on Jeni Lowe's car, causing it to crash. Old man Abercrombie helped her out of the wrecked car. Before she died, she told him about a racket and the name of the man working the racket, who had also fixed her brakes, and that he should inform the police. Abercrombie was also murdered and before he died he said that he tried to get money out of the murderer. He also said he was a monster and that he had a found a money tree. And that's about it.'

Mary thought a moment, then she said, 'Well, how could Abercrombie have extracted money out of him?'

'Blackmail, I expect. He must have told him that he'd better cough up or he'd report the whole thing to the police.'

'Mr Abercrombie must have given the murderer his address.'

'Of course. Abercrombie was no experienced crook.'

'He would have made contact with the murderer by either letter or phone.'

'Must have been by phone because she was murdered on Monday and he was murdered on Wednesday. You know how long the post takes.'

'Hmm. Yes, that's right.'

'Well, you will have checked both his phone and Jeni Lowe's, haven't you?'

'I left Ahmed busy with them. I shan't know what he's found until Monday.'

'Well, *there* you are then,' she said. 'You'll have to relax and forget all about it until Monday.'

He knew she was right. He would try and do just that. 'Yes, love.'

Mary smiled. She stood up. 'Tea will only be a couple of minutes.'

'Good,' he said. Then he remembered the little plastic cap in the bottom of his pocket. 'Just a minute, love,' he said.

She turned and gave him a quizzical look.

He found it and handed it to her. 'That was found under the seat in Jeni Lowe's car. Have you any idea what it is and what it's for?'

She turned it over, held it towards the light, thought a moment then said, 'It can't be the top of a scent bottle because it hasn't any screw thread.'

Angel nodded in agreement.

'Well, then, I've really no idea, Michael,' she said.

'The owner of it is quite probably the murderer of Jeni Lowe and Antony Edward Abercrombie.'

She pulled a shocked face and pushed the gizmo back into his hand. 'Here you are. I don't want it.' Then she added, 'I thought you were going to forget all about work until Monday.'

'I never agreed to it,' he said. 'You suggested it. I made no comment.'

Mary pulled a very serious face. She turned and stood in front of him with her arms akimbo.

Angel pretended to be afraid and in a small voice said, 'But I am willing to give it my most serious attention, your most honourable ladyship.'

'I should think so,' she said, relaxing the stance and turning to go into the kitchen.

'Any post?' Angel said.

'Just one,' she said, taking an envelope off the side-board as she passed it and giving it to him. 'It's from the gas company.'

She went out.

Angel's fists tightened. 'They've not gone and put their ruddy prices up again, have they?'

It was Sunday evening. Angel had remembered that the television programme *Wanna Be Rich?* with Alan de Souza was being transmitted live at 8.30 p.m. Although he rarely watched game shows, he wanted to see it because he had been to the studio and met three of the team involved in the show. Mary agreed, so at the appropriate time he switched on the television and they sat back to watch it.

The dialogue was entirely predictable, and the audience's hands must have been red raw from the number of occasions prearranged and ever-enthusiastic applause was coaxed out of them by a man in a red suit located just out of sight of the cameras.

The woman who had won the most money last week, Josephine Huxley from Birmingham, had returned, hopefully to win more to add to the £62,000 she already had, and was facing two new contestants.

The unseen announcer gave Alan de Souza the most tremendous build-up before he bounced on to the stage in the crispest dinner jacket ever made, smiling and bowing at all the cameras. He introduced the contestants and chatted with them for a few minutes, then began the game. All three contestants answered the first few questions correctly. They were standard general knowledge fodder for quiz enthusiasts. As the programme progressed, the questions became more difficult until by the time the show was transmitting its last segment after the third commercial break, there was only Mrs Huxley from Birmingham remaining and her prize money had risen to £100,000. Then she was to be asked the last question that could potentially increase her prize money to £150,000 or lose her everything — she could leave with nothing and no option to return the following week.

De Souza jacked up the tension by bringing on a soundproof box with a glass window through which the audience could see only her head and shoulders. He asked for quiet so that the contestant would be certain to hear the question clearly.

Fortunately, after some hesitation, she gave the answer to the question and de Souza announced that she had won £150,000 to tremendous applause. He asked her if she wanted to come back the following week and try for £250,000, and she said she would. There was more applause. Then the other two contestants were brought back, given a cheque each for their winnings, more applause, three beautiful girls came on and presented each contestant with a bouquet of flowers, more applause, and that was the end of the show.

Angel pressed the button to switch the TV off. 'What did you think to it?' he said.

Mary yawned. 'Excuse me,' she said, covering her mouth. Then she said, 'It was good for that sort of show.'

'A lot of money, £250,000,' he said. 'It would go a long way to improve *our* circumstances.'

'Yes,' Mary said.

'We could pay off the mortgage,' he said. 'Get a new gas boiler. Repaint the house. Go on a cruise.'

'And I could get some new shoes,' she said.

He looked at her and frowned. He would never understand women. She smiled back at him.

'All right. All right, Mary,' he said. '*If* we had won £250,000, *all* you would have wanted is some new shoes?'

She continued smiling. 'Yes, darling. I didn't say how many pairs.'

It was 8.28 a.m. on Monday, 18 November. It was wet, cold and dull.

Angel arrived at his office as usual.

Before he could take off his coat and hang it up, the phone rang. It was Don Taylor. 'I have a report from our computer expert, sir, about Jeni Lowe's PC.'

Angel's face brightened. 'Yes, lad. What's it say?'

'Well, sir, it says that he has opened all the drives and confirms that the machine appears to have been used exclusively for the preparation of copy for advertisements for clients mostly in the engineering industry and that he couldn't find any notes or comments that might be helpful. He also says that the words "Viktor", "Berezin", "love", "sex", "marriage", "murder" and "kill" are not used anywhere, in any context.'

Angel wrinkled his nose. He had hoped for something useful. 'That sounds pretty conclusive.'

'I'm afraid it does, sir.'

'No point in going down that avenue any further. Anything else?'

'I have Abercrombie's mail, sir. I didn't get round to opening it. It was handed to me by the postman as I was coming away on Friday last. There might be something helpful in there, sir.'

'Right, Don. Send it up.'

There was a knock on the door.

'Come in,' Angel said as he replaced the phone. It was Ahmed. He was carrying a small red evidence bag sealed thoroughly with brown plastic tape.

'Good morning, sir,' Ahmed said. 'This has come by a messenger from Dr Mac.'

'What is it?'

Ahmed placed the bag on the desk.

Angel looked round the bag at a small white label that said, *Contents of pockets of Antony Edward Abercrombie decd.*

Angel's eyebrows went up. He peeled off some of the brown sticky tape, opened the top of the bag and poured the contents out on to his desk.

He went first for the handsome pigskin wallet. He opened it. There were pockets for £20, £10 and £5 notes but they were empty. In a smaller pocket there were five plastic cards. Two were for membership of London clubs, White's and the Reform, both expired in 2006, there was a bank credit card which expired in 2011, a debit card with Coutts & Co., which was still valid, and a card for Tesco's for collecting points.

The other items in the bag consisted of a bunch of keys, a car key for a Jaguar, although he had told Angel he hadn't a car any more, five small coins amounting to 19p, and a handkerchief.

Angel rubbed his chin. The contents told a story: a sad story for old Mr Abercrombie.

'Nothing helpful there, sir?' Ahmed said.

'Unfortunately no,' Angel said and began putting the stuff back into the bag. Ahmed leaned over to help him. As he reached out to pick up the coins, his suit sleeve slipped back a little, revealing the big gold watch.

Angel saw it and grinned. Ahmed noticed that he'd seen it.

'Have you got it telling you the right time yet, lad?' Angel said.

Ahmed smiled. He was pleased it was making an impression on his boss. 'Almost, sir. I've been meaning to ask you something about it.'

'I don't know anything about watches, lad,' he said. 'But if I can help, what is it?'

'Well, sir. I keep setting this watch but I never get it right. It's *Monday* here in the UK, isn't it? When it is six o'clock tea-time, here, today, what day is it in Sydney, Australia?'

Angel frowned. 'Isn't Sydney nine hours ahead of us? That means that at six o'clock here tonight, Monday, it will be three o'clock on *Tuesday* morning in Sydney.'

Ahmed blinked. 'Oh? Thank you, sir.' Then with his fingernails, he pulled a button out of the side of the watch and began turning it. 'It's never right, sir. If I set it right for Sydney, it'll be wrong for Greenwich.'

'I've told you, lad, I'd take it back.'

'I can't, sir. My next-door neighbour did me the most enormous favour letting me have this cheap.'

'Ahmed, whatever price it was, it wasn't cheap enough if it doesn't tell you the right time.'

There was a knock at the door.

'See who that is, lad,' Angel said.

Ahmed opened the door and a PC from SOCO said, 'Package for DI Angel.'

'Who has sent it?' Ahmed said.

'DS Taylor from SOCO.'

'Right, thank you.'

Ahmed took a fat envelope from him, handed it to Angel, closed the door, turned back and said, 'Anything else, sir?'

'Yes,' Angel said, to Ahmed's surprise. 'When are you going to give me the list of calls made by those two phones?'

'Oh, I've finished Jeni Lowe's mobile, sir, but there are a few numbers Mr Abercrombie rang that I can't get a reply from. I may have to go to the phone company and ask them. It shouldn't take long.'

Angel's face brightened. 'Well, let me have Jeni Lowe's straightaway, and crack on with the other. They're both *very* urgent.'

'Right, sir,' he said and went out.

Angel opened the mail that had been intended for Mr Abercrombie. There were four envelopes inside the larger one, and sadly each was a letter asking for payment of a bill of some sort. Two were saying that it was their second time of asking and, in the case of the electricity and gas companies, they were both writing to say that they may have to cut off his supply.

Angel put the letters back in their respective envelopes and pushed them to one side. He could now understand the desperate situation Mr Abercrombie had fallen into. He was still thinking about it when there was a knock at the door.

'Come in.'

It was Ahmed. He was holding two A4 sheets of paper.

'These are the calls made by Jeni Lowe on her mobile, sir,' he said. He put the two pieces of paper on the desk in front of Angel, who eagerly peered down at them.

'You'll see, sir, that the early part of the last two weeks of her life,' Ahmed said, 'she made calls to her parents . . . usually in the evenings, lasting five or ten minutes. Then there were odd calls to shops, and supermarkets . . . then there were calls, one or two a day, to Zenith Studios. As the days passed these calls became more frequent and for longer periods of time.'

Angel's pulse increased. His chest began to buzz. 'So she did have an interest there?' Angel said. 'Hmm. Did you find out who she was speaking to?'

'No, sir. It's a very busy switchboard and they have twenty-four lines. They said they had no idea and there was no way of checking.'

Angel wrinkled his nose.

'Now look at the last few entries, sir,' Ahmed said. 'The day before she died, Saturday. No calls at all to Zenith. Then the day after, Sunday, the *only* call she made was to her parents in Nottingham at four o'clock in the afternoon.'

Angel nodded.

'Does it make any sense to you, sir?'

'I think so, lad,' he said. 'You don't need to phone somebody if you are sat next to them, holding their hand. She had an interest at Zenith all right. I guess a *man*. Although you can never be quite certain these days. She probably was with him all of Saturday and until two or three o'clock on Sunday afternoon. Give her an hour or so to tidy up her mind and think of other things, remember her parents, wonder how they are and give them a ring. Something like that.'

Ahmed beamed. He was glad to be so useful to his boss.

Angel said, 'Now buzz off, there's a good lad, and let me have the same run-down on old man Abercrombie's calls.'

Ahmed grinned. 'Won't be long, sir,' he said, and he went out.

Angel rubbed his chin. He had a great deal of heavy thinking to do. He wanted to try and get into the mind of Jeni Lowe.

His thoughts were full of her when, twenty minutes later, there was a knock on his door.

It was Ahmed carrying a yellow paper file.

'Come in, lad. Have you got Mr Abercrombie's calls?'

'Yes, sir,' Ahmed said as he opened the file on the desk in front of Angel. 'I now know the destination of each call he made during the last two weeks of his life. It's very unusual. All of his calls until Monday, the day Jeni Lowe died, were made to the off-licence, Heneberry's, on Bradford Road.'

'No doubt ordering food and booze,' Angel said. 'I expect they delivered to the door.'

'Then he made only two calls to the Zenith Studios on Monday, and to –'

Angel's eyes lit up. 'I *knew* it, Ahmed!' he said. 'The phone calls are the common denominator. The murderer is somebody who works at Zenith Studios.'

'Looks like it, sir,' Ahmed said. 'I was going to say that he made two calls to Zenith on Monday, three calls on Tuesday, and on Wednesday, the day he died, he made one to Zenith and then one to our number here, sir.'

'Yes, I spoke to him. I remember it well.'

'Then you were the last person he rang before he died, sir.'

Angel's face muscles tightened. He wasn't pleased to have that honour. He might have been able to have saved

Abercrombie's life if he hadn't been delayed by the superintendent. He now knew he should have told the super to go to hell and gone straight down to The Bailiff's House. He *might* have been there in time. But then again, hindsight is a wonderful thing.

'Right, Ahmed. Thank you,' he said.

Ahmed made for the door.

'Just a minute, lad,' Angel said, looking at his watch.

Ahmed turned round.

'Ask DS Carter and DS Crisp to come and see me here at eleven o'clock.'

'Right, sir,' he said.

Angel reached for the phone and said, 'Can you get me the number of the police station in Birmingham Central.'

EIGHT

It was ten minutes past eleven.

In Angel's office with him were DS Carter, DS Crisp and DC Ahaz. They were seated round the desk.

Angel was bringing them up to date with the latest evidence that had come to hand.

'Any more questions?' Angel said.

Nobody said anything.

'Right, well, we know that the murderer is employed at or involved with Zenith Television. Abercrombie's statement, which I have on tape, indicated that the murderer is male. We know that Jeni Lowe had taken to doodling Viktor Berezin's name. It's a clear indication that at some time his name was on her mind but it's difficult to know in what connection. It may have been a romantic notion. It's hard to believe it was an overtly sexual thought. However, Berezin is reputed to be vastly rich. Riches can bring power. Young women can be in love with a powerful man who is also immensely rich. I don't know.'

'Have you any evidence or indications about anybody else, sir?' Flora Carter said.

'No. I have spoken to the three key men on that particular show. Besides Berezin, I have interviewed the presenter,

Alan de Souza, and Dennis Grant, the programme director. As we do not yet know much about either of them, I want to keep a totally open mind.'

Crisp said, 'You mean you don't rule them in and you don't rule them out?'

'Exactly. Now I have a rough plan. Mr Abercrombie in his last words said that the murderer had found a money tree.'

Crisp said, 'What's that, sir?'

'Glad you asked, Trevor. I believe it is a mythological tree that grows money all the time and keeps increasing its yield.'

'That's double-talk for a great racket, isn't it, sir?' Crisp said.

'In this case, it *certainly* is. A money-making racket that gets bigger and bigger, presumably with minimum effort on the part of the villain or villains. Now I want you, Flora, to go to Heneberry's off-licence on Bradford Road. Find out about Abercrombie's relationship with them. What did he buy? Do they deliver down where he lives? Find out when anyone there last saw him and what happened.'

'Right, sir,' she said and stood up.

'Just a minute, Flora. I want you to hear this next bit.'

She sat down.

Angel said, 'We are going to approach this investigation from two directions.' He turned back to Crisp. 'I want you to go down to Birmingham. You might be away for a few nights.'

Crisp's eyebrows shot up. '*Birmingham*, sir?' he said. 'Why Birmingham?'

'I want you to set up a watch on a Mrs Josephine Huxley. She's the current big-money winner on that TV show *Wanna Be Rich?*. I've got her address from Birmingham CID.'

'What has she done, sir?'

'I am not aware that she has done anything, Trevor. She may be as white as the padre's kneecap. That's what I want you to find out. I can tell you that Birmingham police have absolutely nothing on her. And now, of course, they are aware of *our* interest so they will keep well away from her.'

Crisp said, 'When do you want me to go, sir?'

'Now,' Angel said. 'You can take Ted Scrivens with you. He can drive the observation van. You can take your own car. I want you to get her phone bugged and her sitting room or kitchen, wherever she spends most of her time. All right?'

'Is she married, sir?'

Angel tried to hide a smile. 'Trust you to ask a question like that,' he said. 'Birmingham say that there was a man registered on the electoral roll a year last October. But judging from last October's roll, he doesn't seem to be on it now. There is at least one child though. Now off you go. When you get established ring me and let me know. Ahmed's got the address. You can tell Ted Scrivens the good news.'

It was 2 p.m., later that day, Monday, 18 November.

Angel walked up to the pretty girl on the reception desk at Zenith Television and asked for Mr Viktor Berezin.

'Ah, you've been before, Inspector, haven't you? I remember you. You know where the interview rooms are, just round the corner? Would you care to wait in room number one and I'll page him for you?'

Angel made his way round the corner, looking up at the signs on the door. He soon found interview room number one. The door was ajar so he peered inside to check that it wasn't occupied. It wasn't, so he went in and sat down in one of the chairs facing the desk. Minutes later there was a mighty hubbub of screaming and shouting in the hallway outside.

Eventually, the door opened and Berezin looked in. He looked very smart in a well-cut dark suit. However his face suggested that he was not happy; he looked harassed and tired. He transferred the card that read *INTERVIEW IN PROGRESS* from the inside to the outside doorknob and closed the door.

'Ah. Good afternoon, Inspector,' he said as he took the seat behind the desk. 'Have you come to tell me that you have found ze young lady's murderer?'

'I wish I could tell you that, Mr Berezin,' Angel said. 'But I am still making inquiries. That's what brings me back to see you. There is one question I would like to ask.'

'Vot is it, Inspector? I will answer it if I can.'

'Thank you. I would like to ask you about the questions in your show *Wanna Be Rich?*. How many people involved with making the programme have access to the answers?'

'Just about everybody except the contestants. Why?'

'Are the questions and answers not held somewhere safe in secrecy until they are opened in front of the audience by the presenter of the show?'

Berezin smiled. It was a rare occasion and not a pretty sight. His big teeth seemed too large for his small mouth and his face creased, causing his eyes to be reduced to slits.

'I'm afraid not, Inspector,' he said. 'Remember, ze show it is live, so there is no room for mistakes. That opening of the sealed envelopes containing the question and answer is a bit of showmanship to heighten the tension of the show. In truth, there is no secrecy. You see, if the presenter and the crew are not fully aware of the questions and answers at rehearsals, the questions could not be put on the teleprompter, the presenter could not rehearse the pronunciation of any difficult vords, the effects man would not know whether to play the raspberry effect when the answer is wrong or the orchestra chord when it is correct, and it would delay the man who manages the scoreboard making the change after each answer. There are many other reasons. The programme assistants need to check that the easy questions come early in the game, the harder ones later, and they must not seem to be easier or more difficult than any previous game to minimize any sense of unfairness from the audience as well as the contestants. It is this attention to ze detail that makes the show vital and appear so . . . so . . . spontaneous.'

Angel wrinkled his nose. He was not a happy man.

Berezin looked across the desk at him. He waited a second and then said, 'At ze same time, Inspector, I must say that everything is done to make sure that the contestants do not see the answers, of course.'

Angel wondered if that really was a priority. He rubbed his chin. The two victims of murder had both been in touch with somebody at Zenith Television shortly before they were found dead. It was the major similarity in the two murders. It was the common denominator. The girl's doodling of Berezin's name in a way that suggested she was imagining being married to him was another link to Zenith. Ridiculous, of course; he was old enough to be her father and had as much charm as a breeze block. Then Angel recalled that Abercrombie had said that the murderer had found a money tree. Angel knew that he needed to find out where that was. It must be Zenith Television. If he could find it, would it lead him to the identity of the murderer?

'Vell, Inspector, if that is all, you will excuse me. I am up to my shoulders in verk. Was there anything else?'

'Yes. As a matter of fact there is. I need to have an undercover detective on these premises full-time for the next week or so. I have reason to believe that a murder might take place here at any time. Can you organize that?'

Berezin's face looked uglier than ever. He frowned and said, 'Making television programmes is a very creative and expensive business, Inspector, successfully and profitably made by teams of highly experienced men and vimen. It would be a distinct hindrance to be verking with an amateur who has another agenda. Besides, he would stick out like — how do you say it? — like a sore toe.'

'I was thinking of a job in the post room,' Angel said. 'That would allow him to move around the building unchallenged.'

'You really think it's necessary, Inspector?'

'I do, and it would have to be kept absolutely secret for his safety.'

'Our HR department manager would have to know.'

'Right, but nobody else.'

Berezin wasn't happy about the arrangement. He looked down, sighed, shook his head and said, 'Very well. I will arrange it.'

'He can start tomorrow?'

Berezin shrugged. 'Have him report to our HR department tomorrow morning.'

Angel smiled. 'Good. He's a good man. He won't get in your way.'

Berezin looked at his watch. 'Now, is there anything else?'

Angel rubbed his chin. 'Yes. There was something. Oh yes. I would like to know if there is any record of telephone calls coming into the building?'

Berezin frowned. 'I really don't know about that one. You should speak with our floor manager. He knows about the matters like zat. I get him for you.'

'Thank you,' Angel said.

Berezin reached out for the phone on the desk in front of him and tapped in a number. There was no reply. He dialled several different numbers until he caught up with him.

'Morrison?' Berezin said. 'Jed Morrison? . . . I have Detective Inspector Angel of ze police here with me. He would like to see you. Interview room number one . . . Now, I sink.' Eyebrows raised, Berezin looked at Angel.

Angel nodded.

Berezin replaced the phone. 'He'll be two minutes,' he said. 'Now if you will excuse me, Inspector, I must rush. It has been nice meeting you again.'

Angel doubted it. He stood up. They shook hands.

Berezin then left the room, closing the door.

Angel quickly made up his notes and then sat back and waited for Jed Morrison. He hadn't met the man before and he wondered what he was like.

There was a knock at the door and a bronzed, smiling face appeared. 'Inspector Angel?' the young man said.

'That's right,' he said. 'Mr Morrison?'

'Yes, sir,' the tall man said. He had a lot of fair, wavy hair, powerful shoulders and a body to match.

'Come in,' Angel said. 'Please sit down.'

Morrison smiled. When he smiled his whole face lit up. He had charm even when he wasn't trying to be charming. 'What is it you want me for, Inspector?'

'I am investigating the murders of Jeni Lowe and Antony Edward Abercrombie.'

'That's the young lady in the car crash where you come from? Erm, Bromersley? Well, I don't know her. Never met her. I don't understand . . .'

His voice trailed to nothing.

'She was loosely connected to Zenith TV,' Angel said, 'and I'm looking at all the options. I hope you don't mind me asking you one or two questions?'

'No, Inspector Angel, not at all.'

'Good. Good. For instance, where were you last Sunday afternoon and evening?'

Morrison frowned. 'Well, I was here, of course, in Studio Two.'

'All the time? Who was with you?'

'Well, I was checking on all the props and the girls and the flowers and the facilities for the studio audience some of the time. And I was in my office, going through the script, most of the time.'

'Who can verify that, Mr Morrison? Who were you with?'

'I don't suppose anybody could verify it. I was on my own but there were people moving around, checking on the things they were responsible for. It was a live show. Everything had to be just so.'

'I appreciate that, Mr Morrison. But it was possible for you to escape from the hurly-burly of the preparation of the show for a short while, wasn't it?'

'I suppose so, yes. What for?'

'Long enough to have interfered with the brakes on Jeni Lowe's car.'

His face changed. His big blue eyes stuck out as if they were on bilberry stalks. '*What?*' he said. 'I don't even *know* the girl. Or which one was her car. And, anyway, why should I?'

Angel smiled but it wasn't a warm smile. 'Exactly,' he said. 'Why should you?'

Jed Morrison looked perplexed.

'That's the answer I would have given, Mr Morrison,' Angel said. 'As long as the investigator doesn't know the motive for the crime, he can't solve the mystery, can he?'

'But I *didn't* know her, Inspector. I *didn't* murder her.'

'Do you know *why* she was murdered?'

'No. What makes you think her murder has anything to do with me?'

'I'll tell you. It was a doodle on her notebook . . . a man's name . . . linked with hers.'

'It wasn't my name. It couldn't have been.'

'And then there were phone calls from both victims to someone here . . . both timed at shortly before they died. Were they to you?'

'Certainly not. I don't know anything about any phone calls.'

'Where were you last Wednesday afternoon?'

'I don't know. I'd have to think. Last Wednesday afternoon . . . That was the thirteenth. I was here. I had a meeting in the morning with Viktor Berezin about a new show he is considering . . . it dragged on a bit . . . went straight through lunch. Grabbed a sandwich and a coffee about three o'clock, then went to my office and caught up with my paperwork until around five o'clock. Then I went home.'

'Was anybody with you when you were at your desk?'

'You mean, have I got an alibi?' He shook his head. 'No, Inspector. I was on my own from about three o'clock. Maybe somebody saw me through the office window. I don't know.'

Angel wrinkled his nose. Then he searched around in his coat pocket for the little blue plastic cover or top. He held it up between finger and thumb. 'Do you know what this is?'

Morrison took it, looked at it, frowned and handed it back. 'No idea, Inspector.'

'Ever seen it before?' Angel said.

'Not to my knowledge,' Morrison said.

Angel stuffed it back into his pocket.

'Mr Morrison,' Angel said. 'Is there any way in which I can check on phone calls coming into Zenith Television?'

Morrison thought a moment. 'No, Inspector, I don't think there is,' he said. 'The only way it could be done is for the switchboard operators to write down every call that came in, but they get thousands in a day, and there doesn't seem to be any need for it.'

Angel wasn't surprised but he was disappointed. 'Right, Mr Morrison,' he said. 'Thank you.'

The chiming clock in the hall at The Brambles struck four o'clock. The sky was colourful even though it was becoming dark. Cora Blenkinsop had already left for home and Helen Rose was alone in the kitchen preparing tea for her husband Paul and herself. She discovered that the last three slices of a loaf of bread had green mould on the crust, so she cut the bread up roughly into cubes and scraped it on to a plate. Then she looked outside down the garden at the bird table. It was in an open area of grass in the midst of trees at the side of the old slaughterhouse. The wintry sky beyond was red and gold and purple. The trees stripped of leaves stood starkly in silhouette.

She went into the hall, put her coat on over her overalls, kicked off her slippers and put on some old shoes. She returned to the kitchen, collected the plate of bread and went outside.

It was cold but there was no wind and no rain.

As she approached the bird table, she noticed how slippery it was underfoot. She looked down and discovered she was walking on sodden leaves, which was not surprising considering the number of trees there were in the garden and the woods beyond, and the recent weather.

She reached the bird table and hurriedly tipped the bread on to it, then took the plate to the back step of the house to collect when she went in. She wanted it safe. It had been a wedding present and she didn't want it broken. Then she went down the path to the old slaughterhouse. It was not until she reached the door that the fear of the history of the Cudlipps, never far away from her, returned. Nevertheless she pressed on. She needed the stiff yard brush that was in the slaughterhouse and she intended getting it. She pushed open the heavy wooden door and looked into the dark building. She could just make out forks, rakes and other tools hanging on the wall. She spotted the brush, reached out for it, lifted it up, turned and quickly left, pulling the door after her. Her breathing returned to normal as she went up the unmade path towards the bird table. The brushing quickly removed the leaves and unexpectedly exposed a straight line of irregular white stones, each about the size of a tea plate, more than five feet in length. She followed the line and brushed clear the next stone to reveal more stones ahead, but also to the left and to the right. She kept brushing the leaves away until she revealed the shape of a cross. Then it dawned on her. She gasped and put her hand to her face. She had unsuspectingly uncovered the burial place of Amos Cudlipp. Her breathing increased. Her heart began to race. Her immediate impulse was to cover up the stones. But she dropped the brush, ran quickly to the back door, let herself in, locked the door and stood with her back to it until she decided what to do. Her first instinct was to ring the garage where her husband worked and ask the manager to let him come home . . . but she would look so stupid and clinging . . . she couldn't do that. Her eyes flitted from left to right and she lightly squeezed the flesh under her nose between finger and thumb for a few moments as she thought. Then she made a decision.

She raced round the house and switched on the lights in every room. Then she took off her coat, changed into her slippers and returned to the kitchen. She looked at the clock. It was a quarter to five. Paul would be home in half an hour.

The phone rang. It rang loudly. Imperatively. She wasn't expecting anyone to call.

She made her way into the hall and picked it up. It was Paul.

She sighed with relief. It was so good to be able to talk to him. 'Oh, hello, darling, so pleased to hear your voice.'

'Why?' he said. 'What's the matter?'

'Nothing,' she said. 'It's just lovely to hear you. I haven't heard you since breakfast.'

Paul Rose laughed. 'And it's lovely to hear you too,' he said. 'Look, darling, things have gone a bit pear-shaped here today. Promises have been made that shouldn't have been and the long and short of it is that I've got to get a car finished tonight because the customer needs it first thing in the morning. So I'm going to be at least an hour late . . . thought I'd let you know so that you wouldn't be worried.'

Helen wasn't pleased, but it *was* work. What could she do? 'Never mind, love,' she said. 'I'll hold tea back. Just come as soon as you can. And I love you.'

'Certainly will, my darling. And I love you too. Byeeee.'

'Goodbye, my darling.'

NINE

It was 4.45 when Angel arrived back at his office. He was about to summon Ahmed when there was a knock at the door.

'Come in,' he called. It was Flora.

'I've just come back from Heneberry's off-licence, sir. Thought you might want to hear about it — if it's convenient?'

'Oh yes? Sit down, lass. What did you find out?'

'They were sorry to hear of Mr Abercrombie's death, sir. They genuinely liked the old boy, who they had known many years. He seemed to buy ninety-nine per cent of his food and bits and pieces from them. They used to deliver his main order on a Friday morning, but were often put to the trouble of bringing oddments he had run out of at other times in the week. And they were not pleased that he had run up a bill of £300, which might not get paid.'

'Understandably.'

'The last time anyone saw him was Tuesday last when Mr Heneberry himself delivered some oddments to his house, including a bottle of whisky.'

Angel frowned. 'Just a minute, Flora,' he said. 'When did I see him the first time? It was Monday, a week today. He said somewhat shamefacedly that he didn't have any booze in the house. That's right. It fits. Carry on, Flora.'

'Mr Heneberry said that he had a go at Mr Abercrombie about settling his bill. Apparently Abercrombie said that he was expecting a lot of money coming to him very soon and that he would easily be able to clear his bill, and that he — Mr Heneberry — wasn't to worry about it.'

Angel rubbed his chin. 'That's interesting, Flora. That he said he was coming into a lot of money. You know, although I didn't really know old Mr Abercrombie, I don't think he uttered one lie to me. He even admitted that he had stolen Jeni's money and valuables after she had died.'

'But that's despicable, sir.'

'It is. But he *was* desperate. If Heneberry's had called in their debt, he could have been declared bankrupt. Then where would he be? His pride wouldn't have survived it.'

'It's no excuse.'

'No, but it makes it understandable. Jeni Lowe told him who had interfered with her brakes, as well as the stuff about the money tree racket.' He bit his bottom lip and shook his head. 'If only he had told me.'

There was a knock at the door.

'Come in,' he called.

It was Ahmed.

'Ah, come in, lad. Just the one I want to see.'

Ahmed grinned. He wasn't used to such a greeting.

Flora Carter stood up. 'Well, I'll be going, sir, unless you want me.'

He looked across at her. 'Anything more to tell me about Heneberry's?'

'No, sir,' she said.

He nodded and she went out.

Angel turned to Ahmed and said, 'Now, lad, what did you want with me?'

'DS Taylor phoned this afternoon while you were out, sir. He said I was to tell you that the prints on the whisky bottle found at the scene of Jeni Lowe's murder were those of Abercrombie. Of course it will be confirmed in his report but he thought you might like to know in advance.'

Angel's screwed up his face in thought. 'I see,' he said. 'Hmm. I see. Well, it only confirms what we already know, that Abercrombie was on the scene and so on. Right. Thank you, Ahmed. Make a point of thanking DS Taylor for me, will you?'

'Yes, of course, sir. Now you said you wanted *me* for something?'

'Yes. How would you like an undercover job?'

The young man's eyes lit up. 'What do you mean, sir?'

'I've got a job for you in the post room at Zenith Television, Leeds. Report to their Human Resources department at 8.30 tomorrow morning and don't be late.'

'Wow! Sir.'

Helen Rose was in the kitchen at The Brambles setting the table. The Westminster chiming clock in the hall struck five. She made a quick calculation and worked out that Paul wouldn't be home from the garage for seventy-five minutes. She wasn't pleased. Seventy-five minutes could drag like hell. She was still on edge but feeling better than she had been an hour earlier.

She peered in the oven at the casserole. It was very gently bubbling so she turned it down to slow cook. Then she checked the table. Everything seemed all right there.

She went into the hall and happened to notice that the landing and all the rooms up there still had their lights on from her panic attack an hour earlier. She pursed her lips. It wouldn't do for Paul to see what she had felt a need to do. He might think she was going out of her mind. She switched off all the unnecessary lights downstairs and then those upstairs. After that, she went into the bedroom, and a heavy gust of rain drummed loudly on the glass panes of the big window. She quickly closed the curtains, cutting out the rainstorm and the darkness. Then she crossed to the dressing table, sat down on the kidney-shaped dressing table stool and looked in the mirror. She began to brush her hair but soon became impatient — it wouldn't quite stay how she wanted it. She worked diligently until she had the curls and waves in the right place, then reached out to the back of the dressing table for the hairspray. She approved of the result. It was much better. As she returned the container of lacquer to the back of the dressing table, out of the corner of her eye, in the mirror, she saw a piece of white lace or tulle or similar, like the bottom of an old-fashioned dress, disappear rapidly under the edge of the wardrobe door, which was open two or three inches. It then closed with a click.

She froze to the spot. For a second or two she held her breath. There was only the sound of rain on the bedroom window. Her heart was pounding like a steam engine. She could not move. Her eyes were still glued to the mirror, watching to see if there was any further movement. She began to breathe rapidly. Then she suddenly jumped up, crossed quickly to the landing, raced down the stairs and straight out of the back door. All she could think about was putting distance between herself and the house.

Rain was tumbling down as though a cloud had burst.

She ran down the path, through the gate and into the road, totally oblivious to anything.

The headlights of a car, travelling at around 30 miles an hour, was the only illumination of the normally deserted road. The driver braked. She ran into the side of it even though it was still moving. The impact of her body on the bonnet and wheel arch made the loud echoing noise of a man kicking a drum. She bounced back off the bonnet and landed in the gutter.

Angel pressed on the car's emergency flashers, pulled the BMW into the nearside, picked up the police-issue rubber-covered torch off the dashboard shelf and quickly got out.

The woman was several yards behind the car in the gutter. He shone the torch in her face. Her eyes were closed. She didn't move. Angel thought she was dead. Then he saw her chest heave and her eyes open.

'Are you all right?' he said.

She looked in every direction. 'Who are you?' she said.

'Detective Inspector Angel,' he said. 'Are you all right? You ran into my car.'

She put her hand to her face. She remembered the vision of the dress in the wardrobe door and groaned.

'Oh, dear. Oh, yes.'

'Are you all right?' he said. 'Can you stand up?'

'I think so.'

'I'll help you,' he said, putting his hand under her arm. 'Have you any pain anywhere?'

'No. No, I don't think so.'

Angel pulled her up hard. She was on her feet.

'Where do you live?'

She turned her head round and looked upwards.

Light shone from some of the windows of The Brambles.

She shuddered and said, 'Up there.'

'Come on,' he said. 'I'll help you home.'

Her eyes flashed. 'No. I can't go back there.'

A rain cloud seemed to open directly above them.

Angel said, 'Well, let's get you into the car.'

He held her under her arm, opened the nearside front door, helped her inside and closed the door. He noticed how wet her clothes were and that she wasn't wearing a coat of any kind.

He rushed round the car and climbed in behind the steering wheel.

'I should take you round to the hospital, check you are all right.'

'I'm fine. Thank you very much. You are very kind.'

'You don't want to go back home?'

'*No,*' she said promptly. 'Not until my husband arrives.'

'I don't think you should sit in those wet clothes for long. I live only a mile away. Shall I take you to my house? My wife will be there and she will be able to . . . well, it will be warm and dry there.'

Before she had time to protest, Angel had turned the ignition key and started the car engine.

'More coffee, Helen?' Mary said.

'No, thank you. You've both been extremely kind. I ought to be getting back. I'd rather my husband didn't know how silly I've been.'

'You could phone him and see how close he is to finishing,' Mary said.

'Yes, if you don't mind, I will,' she said, finishing off her coffee and returning the cup to the tray.

'The phone's in the hall,' Mary said. 'Come on. I'll show you.'

'And I'll take you home, when you're ready,' Angel said.

'He's bound to be suspicious when he sees you in my clothes,' Mary said, as she led the way out of the sitting room into the hall.

Helen Rose smiled as she followed her. 'I don't know,' she said. 'I don't think he notices what I'm wearing, and your clothes are all a pretty good fit. I'll be certain to launder them and return them to you tomorrow, and I am eternally grateful.'

'There's no rush at all.'

Mary returned to the sitting room as Helen Rose used the phone. Her face showed her concern and compassion for the newlywed. She looked at Angel and they exchanged smiles.

Five minutes later, Angel stopped the BMW at the back gate of The Brambles. A happier and dryer Helen Rose got out. Angel opened the boot and took out a plastic bag containing her clothes.

'I'll take that, thank you,' she said, reaching out for the bag. 'And thank you very much again. And thank Mary again for me.'

'Will you be all right? Do you want me to come in and wait until your husband comes?'

'No. I'll be all right now. But thank you. Please go. If he sees you, he'll ask questions and I don't want that.'

Angel nodded. 'Good night then,' he said and returned to the car.

'Good night,' she said and waved him off.

Angel was soon back at home. He put the car away and let himself in through the back door.

Mary was looking in the oven. 'I don't know what this'll be like,' she said.

Angel took off his jacket and put it on the newel post in the hall. He came back to the kitchen, rolling up his shirt sleeves.

'Did you see the husband then? Love's young dream?' Mary said.

'She didn't want me to see him,' he said as he began washing his hands under a running tap.

'They're very much in love, don't you think?' she said as she served something from a dish on to two plates.

He dried his hands, pursed his lips and said, 'Aye. Well, *she* is. I only hope he warrants it.'

She put the plates on the table. 'You said that seriously. Is something bothering you?'

He looked at his plate and frowned. 'What is this?' he said.

'What does it look like?' she said. 'Dried-up steak and kidney, overboiled potatoes and carrots, Sherlock.'

He stuck a fork into the steak. 'I don't think it's likely that the three different "visions" or "events" would come entirely from her imagination. When she is normal, that is to say when she is not afraid, she doubts the veracity of what she has said.'

'She begins to doubt herself.'

'Exactly. Yet she is perfectly normal to talk to.'

'Perfectly,' she said.

She saw Angel having a tussle with a piece of steak. 'Sorry it's dry, Michael. I can make some gravy?'

'Don't bother, love. But I have had three rounds with this piece,' he said, pushing the gristle to the edge of his plate. 'I will have to throw in the towel.'

They ate in silence for a few moments, then Mary said, 'What are the *three* "events" or manifestations of ghostly activity you referred to, love?'

Angel stopped loading his fork. 'Well, the business tonight of the woman disappearing into the wardrobe, the inability of her and her help, Cora Blenkinsop, to light a real fire in the room downstairs, and the man in a stovepipe hat bearing down on her in her back yard, believed to be Amos Cudlipp.'

'Mmm. I see. And do you believe that gory tale about Amos Cudlipp?'

'I have heard that there *was* such a character living there some time back. *That* story could all be true, love. Those are facts that can be verified. I don't know what to think about all the other stuff.'

'Are you suggesting she's making it up?'

'Well, I don't know. She needs help of some sort. I would have liked to have looked in her wardrobe earlier this evening.'

Mary pulled a face. 'Not me,' she said with a shudder. She put her fork down and concentrated on chewing, then swallowed a piece of steak. After that she said, 'Should she see a psychiatrist?'

'I wouldn't go that far at this stage, but have you noticed her husband is never around when these ghostly manifestations occur?'

'Whatever you say, Michael, I believe *her,*' she said. 'Ghosts, if there are such phenomena, can't be explained by forensic experts and policemen.'

'No, but *fake* ghosts can,' he said. 'Look at the situation as it is. A young man marries an older woman for her money, then when they've been married a short time, a young bit of fluff takes his eye. And he fancies taking her to bed rather than his older wife. How is he going to arrange it?'

'Well, the days are gone when he could have his wife consigned to a private mental asylum.'

'Aye,' Angel said. 'The easy way is kill her off and make it look like an accident.'

'Is that what you think Paul Rose wants to do?'

'I don't know. Never met the man.'

'You *are* ghoulish.'

TEN

It was half past eight on Tuesday, 19 November.

Angel was at his desk fingering through the huge pile of mail and paperwork — the blight of every policeman's life — when there was a knock at the door.

'Come in,' he called.

The door opened and the pretty face and shapely figure of PC Leisha Baverstock, the station beauty, appeared. She was the woman who was having an on-off relationship with DS Crisp, which Angel could not keep up with nor comprehend.

'Good morning, sir,' she said. 'I got a message to say that you wanted me.'

'You may know that DC Ahmed Ahaz is away for me on an undercover job.'

She smiled and said, 'Yes, sir. He's been round everybody telling us about it. It's in the post room at Zenith Television.'

Angel was surprised that the PC knew, and he wasn't too pleased. 'It's supposed to be an undercover job, Leisha. You'll keep that information to yourself, won't you?'

'Yes, sir. But it's all round the station. He was so proud.'

'I understand,' Angel said. 'Now while he is away, I want you to stand in his shoes. When I'm out, I want *you* to take my messages, all right?'

She smiled broadly. 'Oh *yes,* sir.'

Angel scratched his head, then said, 'You'll need to tell the switchboard, the post room, the duty sergeant, DS Taylor at SOCO and anybody else who you think might need to know. All right?'

'Right, sir,' she said.

'And there's something I want you to do for me. There's a house called The Brambles on Havercroft Lane, off Sheffield Road. I want you to ring round the estate agents and see if you can find out who had it on their books and sold it recently to a Mr and Mrs Paul Rose. All right?'

'Yes, sir,' she said. She made some hieroglyphics on her notepad.

'And I want you to go on to the PNC and find out if there's anything known of a Cora Blenkinsop. She'll be between twenty and forty years of age. I don't know where she lives, but she must live locally. All right?'

'All right, sir,' she said. She made some more hieroglyphics then left.

Angel smiled and returned to wading through the pile.

A few moments later, there was a knock on the door again.

'Come in,' he said.

It was PC Leisha Baverstock again. She held out a yellow paper file.

He looked up. That was quick, he thought.

'There were these notes I found on Ahmed's desk, sir. They looked important.'

Angel took the file. It was a report from Martin Edwards, the sergeant in charge of the Motor Vehicles section. It was marked for DI Angel's attention. He opened the file.

'Thank you, Leisha.'

Angel began to read Sergeant Edwards' detailed report on Jeni Lowe's car. He already knew the pertinent facts about the cause of the crash, the damage, the finding of the blue plastic cap under the nearside front seat and the discovery of fresh fingerprints lifted from inside the car. What he didn't know was the identity of the person. The report said that the fingerprints were not those of Antony Edward Abercrombie, 'known to be associated with the case', nor were they available at records, so Angel knew the person had not been through the criminal system.

He eased back in the swivel chair and rubbed his chin.

The phone rang.

'Angel,' he said.

'It's Trevor Crisp, sir, reporting in.'

Angel leaned back into the swivel chair. 'Good lad. Have you found the woman's house?'

'Yes, sir. It's a semi-detached, small garden, on the leafy outskirts of Brum. There's hundreds of them. All look the same. We're in the van and parked at the opposite side of the road to where she lives. Camera is all set up. We've been here about an hour. Haven't seen a person who could be Josephine Huxley yet. Or anyone else in the house, if there is anybody in.'

'Right, Trevor. Is Scrivens all right?'

'Yes, sir. At the minute he's got binoculars on the windows hoping to get a glimpse of life.'

'Hmm. Well, you know what you have to do? Don't take any stupid risks.'

'Oh no, sir. We'll wait for an opportunity.'

'Right, lad,' Angel said. 'I'll leave it with you. Ring me when you have anything to report.'

He replaced the phone. It immediately rang again.

He snatched it up. 'Angel,' he said.

It was Superintendent Harker.

'Angel, I want you up here straightaway,' he said.

'Right, sir,' Angel said.

Harker banged down the phone.

Angel wasn't pleased. He looked as if he'd caught the smell of the gravy in the cook house in Strangeways.

He replaced the phone and pushed the chair away from the desk. He wondered what Harker wanted. It was never anything pleasant. Always a grumble; never appreciation or thanks.

He trudged up the corridor to the door, knocked on it and then pushed it open. He was met with the usual menthol-smelling fug.

'There you are,' Harker said from behind the barricade of files, letters, reports, boxes of Kleenex, Movicol and Co-codamol. 'Sit down,' he said, pointing to the chair opposite. 'I've been trying to keep abreast of your progress, or lack of it, with the murders of this young woman Lowe and the man Abercrombie, and I don't understand why on earth you have sent Ahaz undercover to the television company. We are very short-staffed here, and I am not certain that that was at all necessary. Are you still trying to edge your way into becoming a television star? You'll be doing commentaries and documentaries on crime for them next, like that man, years ago, Edgar Lustgarten.'

'Nothing could be further from the truth, sir. There is enough evidence to indicate that the murderer is a member of the staff of a particular programme made and transmitted by the company. That's all.'

'If you are referring to the scribble on the victim's notepad at her place of work . . . ?'

'There's more than that, sir. It's all in my report.'

'Ah yes, the phone calls from both victims to the TV company's switchboard? I don't suppose you have been able to find out the recipient of the calls? I bet we've all phoned the TV company with some query or complaint over the years. That's probably what's happened.'

'It's tenuous, sir, I admit, but it's all I've got.'

Harker stuck out his chest; it wasn't much bigger than a budgerigar's. 'You'll have to be careful, lad, or you're going to lose your golden-boy status with the press.'

Angel's lips tightened. 'I don't know *what* you mean, sir,' he said. But of course he did. He was used to being insulted by the superintendent. As a mere detective inspector, it went with the job. Up to that present day, he had solved every murder case on his patch, and the appreciation from the innocent involved in the cases, the rest of the force, the public and the media more than compensated for the barbs and petty insults he endured from Superintendent Harker. One day, however, Angel feared that he was going to fail to find the murderer, and he lived in dread of it.

'And another thing,' Harker said. 'What's the idea of sending two men, one of them a sergeant, all the way to Birmingham on inquiries? We do enough inquiries for Birmingham for them to be pleased, nay, eager to do inquiries for us, and on a quid pro quo basis.'

'The inquiries are too complex and too extensive for a simple inquiry to be commissioned, sir. Birmingham have already found and supplied us with the address of the woman we are interested in.'

'I shouldn't think that would tax them overmuch with their budget. What are you wanting Crisp and Scrivens to find out that is beyond Birmingham CID?'

'It's not beyond them, sir. It might be complicated and wide ranging. I want my men to make covert inquiries about a contestant, Josephine Huxley, who is running up big winnings on the quiz show *Wanna Be Rich?*.'

Harker's eyes flashed. 'What?' he said. 'That means there'll be accommodation for the two men, meals in fancy restaurants, petrol hither and thither . . .' The colour in his face drained away.

'Well, er, yes, sir,' Angel said.

'Your men eat like prize-fighters when they're on expenses and overweight jockeys when they're at home. All I can say is that this expedition of yours had better show some results very soon. Right. I'm very busy searching for a Father Christmas for the ACPO children's party. Off you go. I hope to see somebody charged with murder in the very near future.'

Angel left the superintendent's office, cursing and swearing under his breath all the way down the corridor. By the time he was back in his chair in his own office, he was feeling much better.

PC Leisha Baverstock knocked on the door.

Angel looked across at her. 'What is it, lass?'

'I've found the estate agent who sold The Brambles on Havercroft Lane to Mrs Rose, sir,' she said.

Angel's face brightened. 'Oh? Great stuff,' he said and reached out for his pen.

'It's Ackroyd and Whitehouse, sir. And their phone number is 223942.'

'Thank you, Leisha.'

She smiled, went out and closed the door.

He had heard of them. They were an old-established, ostensibly respectable firm with an office on a side street in the centre of Bromersley. He reached out for the phone and tapped in the number and was soon speaking to the man in charge, Archie Ackroyd.

'I understand that you sold a house called The Brambles recently?' Angel said.

'Yes, a Regency stone-built gentleman's residence with several interesting features. I sold it to a Mrs Helen Rose, who had recently married.'

Angel blinked. 'To *Mrs* Rose?'

'Yes, that's right. A very charming lady,' Ackroyd said. 'What is your interest, Inspector?'

Angel pursed his lips. 'Didn't a villain called Amos Cudlipp live there?'

'Many, many years ago. He had the house built for himself and his child bride in or about 1740.'

'Oh? What else can you tell me about him?'

Ackroyd told him the entire horrific story through to Cudlipp being found dead in the River Don.

Angel listened carefully.

When he had finished, Ackroyd said, 'What's your interest in the property, Inspector?'

'These are just inquiries of a private nature, Mr Ackroyd,' he said, not wanting to give anything away. 'Who was the vendor in the sale to Mrs Rose?'

'Let me see,' Ackroyd said. 'It was sold to close the estate of Hubert Grant. If you remember he had a shop in town called Aladdin's Cave.'

'Ah yes,' he said. 'I remember it well. It began as an antique shop, but it sold all sorts of curios and unusual things. He used to buy from the public as well. He had a big sign on the front of the shop that said, "I buy owt".'

'That's right. His house and contents were sold under the instruction of his daughter, Mrs Malwhinney. The contents were sold by us by auction in September last. Did very well, I recall.'

'Have you got an address for her?'

'I'm just looking it up, Inspector. Let me see . . . yes, here it is. It's Mrs Vera Malwhinney, The Coach House, Liddle Lane, Puddleton, Bromersley.'

'Thank you very much, Mr Ackroyd, goodbye.'

Angel replaced the phone.

He rubbed his chin. He knew Puddleton was a pretty hamlet on the Wakefield side of Bromersley, about four miles away. He decided he would visit her. He reached out for his hat and coat and was soon on his way.

Angel found The Coach House hidden away behind bushes and trees at the end of a long single-track lane.

He drove the BMW up to the front door, got out and pressed the bell-push. He could hear it ring in the distance. He stood on the boot-scraping grid and waited. He pressed the bell-push again and it was eventually opened by a powerful-looking Chinese man in a crisp white shirt buttoned up to the neck, black trousers and red braces.

He scowled at Angel and growled something that sounded like, 'Mnya?'

Angel took him to be a sort of butler-type character, produced a card and gave it to him. 'I would like to see Mrs Vera Malwhinney, please,' he said.

The man took the card, bowed, growled, 'Mnya, myna,' and closed the door.

Angel was surprised to have the door closed in his face. He looked up at the grey November sky and hoped it wouldn't rain before he was admitted.

Another few minutes and the door opened. The man stood back and gestured for Angel to enter. He was directed by hand signals and grunts to go along a long corridor at the side of the house. He went through several rooms which were delightfully furnished and eventually was directed into a big room that housed a large blue swimming pool with a domed glass roof above it. A blonde woman in a two-piece bathing costume was making a strong swim away from him. She turned quickly at the far end and swam back to the corner of the pool where the steps were and where Angel was standing. She stopped swimming, looked up at him, her feet found the steps and she walked majestically out of the pool.

Angel thought she looked in great shape.

She looked Angel up and down. 'I won't keep you a moment, Inspector,' she said.

Angel nodded.

She was met on the top step of the pool by the Chinese man, who was carrying a pair of rubber shoes, a white bathrobe and a towel. He assisted her in putting on the bathrobe then went out. Meanwhile she swept up the long blonde locks and in a couple of deft moves rolled them all into a turban.

'This way,' she said and she went through a door into a gymnasium where there were half a dozen exercise machines, lined up against a wall, facing a giant TV screen and a massage table.

The man was opening two sun chairs and setting them by a small occasional table by the window.

'Thank you, Charles,' she said. Then she turned to Angel and said, 'Please sit down. Would you care to join me in a small brandy? I always have a drink after a swim.'

Angel smiled. 'No, thank you,' he said.

Mrs Malwhinney held up one finger and said, 'Just the one, Charles, please.'

The man nodded, grunted and went out.

Angel watched Charles leave.

'Now, Inspector, what can I do for you?' she said.

Angel turned back to face her. He was rubbing his chin.

'I suppose you are wondering about Charles?' she said.

Angel hesitated, then shrugged.

'It's not difficult to explain. My late husband Edwin engaged him when we lived in Hong Kong, then when we needed to come back to UK, Charles came with us. Shortly after that, my husband died and Charles and I had become — shall we say — used to each other. He didn't want to go back so he stayed with me. He's an excellent cook but his real expertise is massage. He has the most healing hands I know. He knows exactly where to press his thumbs. And he's a most excellent houseman and loyal bodyguard.'

Angel smiled and nodded.

'Now it's your turn, Inspector. What do you want from me?'

'Answers to a few questions, Mrs Malwhinney, if you don't mind. I understand that you were the executor of a trust that owned The Brambles on Havercroft Lane in Bromersley?'

'Yes, that's right,' she said. 'My father bought the house more than thirty years ago. It was in trust for my mother but she died in 1999 and my father died in August last.'

'I understand that the house was sold to a Mr and Mrs Paul Rose recently?'

'Well, yes, I understand that it was, Inspector — why?'

Charles arrived with a small tray with a glass of brandy on it. He put the glass on the table and went out.

'Did you ever live there?'

'I spent all my life there until I got married at twenty-four,' she said. She reached out for the glass, took a sip, then swigged the rest in one swallow.

'I understand that Amos Cudlipp committed several horrific murders there.'

'Oh yes, Inspector. It's true. I've had that story told to me many a time.'

'While you were living there, did you see anything spooky or experience anything unusual, that couldn't be explained?'

She grinned. 'You mean the appearance of a man in a stovepipe top hat carrying a huge knife, and a young girl in a long dress coming out of the wardrobe?'

Angel's face brightened. 'Yes?'

'No,' she said. 'There were stacks of horror stories of that sort going round. I never saw *anything*. It might have been rather fun if I had.'

He blinked, then frowned. 'What about your father and mother?' he said.

'They never saw anything either. Not to my knowledge. We weren't that sort of people, Inspector.'

Angel pursed his lips.

'Why, Inspector, has it come up that somebody has seen something?' she asked.

'Yes. Mrs Rose has been made very upset apparently. There's just one more question. There's a small room near the front door.'

'Yes. Dad used to use it as a sort of study or office.'

'That would be the room. When you were there, how was it heated?'

'As a young girl, we had gas central heating installed throughout the house. There's a radiator in there under the window. That provided background heat but in the winter Dad used to have a two-bar electric fire in there also.'

'Thank you very much, Mrs Malwhinney.'

ELEVEN

Leisha Baverstock knocked on the door, opened it and peered into Angel's office. 'You wanted me, sir,' she said.

'Yes, Leisha,' he said. 'Got your notebook?'

'Yes, sir.'

'Right. Come in. Sit down. I want you to find out if anything is known of a woman called Vera Malwhinney or Vera Grant, Edwin Malwhinney, Hubert Grant and a Chinese man with the unlikely name of Charles.'

Leisha frowned. 'Charles what?'

'Just Charles, lass,' he said. 'That's all I know. There can't be many Chinese in Bromersley called Charles.'

She wrote something else in her notebook.

He felt in his jacket pocket and found the blue plastic cap that he had been carrying around for the last few days. He took it out and held it between his second finger and thumb.

'Have you any idea what this is, Leisha? It was found under the seat of Jeni Lowe's car. The owner of it is her murderer and the murderer of old Mr Abercrombie.'

She took it from him and had a good look at it.

'It's from the top of something, sir . . . to keep the dust out,' she said, then she handed it back.

'We know that, but what?' he said.

She shook her head. 'I've no idea, sir.'

Angel slipped the thing back into his pocket.

Then she said, 'Now you asked me to find out if anything is known about a Cora Blenkinsop.'

His face lit up. 'Oh yes. What have you got?'

She turned back a page of her notebook.

'There's nothing at all about her on the PNC, sir, but there are some Blenkinsops known who live at 102 Canal Road. There's a Lionel Blenkinsop, born 1962, who has served four years, from 2001 to 2005, for forging vehicle registration books, assaulting a police officer and resisting arrest.'

Angel pulled a face. 'Oh yes, I remember him now. Nasty piece of work.'

'Also Selina Blenkinsop, born 1965, who served two years, from 2001 to 2003, for passing stolen vehicle registration books.'

'Oh, I remember her too, of course.'

'I then checked that Canal Road address with the electoral roll and found that in addition to Lionel and Selina Blenkinsop, a Cora Angelina Blenkinsop born 1984 also lives there. I assume that that is the woman you wanted me to check on?'

'It certainly is, Leisha,' he said. 'And with a family background like that, she is definitely worth a visit.'

It was twenty minutes to five and the sky was growing dim when Angel pulled on the handbrake of the BMW outside 102 Canal Road. A cold wind blew along the deserted street; the stray dogs who usually perambulated the area in daylight hours must have found warmer, more hospitable places to inhabit.

Number 102 was a terraced house on the cobbled street, one of several hundred built near the canal around 1904 by coal mine owners for their workers.

As Angel climbed out of the car and looked round, a dozen or so houses showed light from their cosy but poky front rooms, and four from their upper front floor bedrooms, but there were no other signs of life.

There was a street lamp outside number 102, as there was intermittently along the long rows of houses, but none were lit, and when Angel shone his torch at the top of the lamppost, he noted that all the glass had been systematically removed, probably by catapult or airgun.

He reached up to the knocker of 102 and banged it deliberately four times. A few moments later light shone through the front room window on to the flagstones and cobbles. Then he heard the sliding of a bolt and the turn of a key. The door was opened and a big man appeared.

Angel recognized him immediately.

'What do you want?' the big man said.

'Well, well, well,' Angel said. 'It's Mr Lionel Blenkinsop.'

'Who the 'ell did you expect to see, Lady bleeding Gaga?'

'It's Inspector Angel, Bromersley police.'

'That's a surprise. I thought it was Father bleeding Christmas coming early to bring me a present. Well, go away. I'm having my tea.'

'It's not you I want to see, Lionel.'

'Selina's having her tea as well.'

'It's your daughter, Cora Angelina Blenkinsop, I want to see.'

'Well, she won't want to see you. You've nothing on her. She's as clean as Snow White.'

A gust of cold wind blew up some dust and a discarded fish and chip paper off the pavement around Angel's feet.

Blenkinsop said, 'It's blowing cold air in here. I gotta close this door.' He began to push it to.

'Just a minute, Dad,' a woman's voice said from behind him.

Blenkinsop stopped and turned.

A head of hair appeared under his arm. It looked up at Angel.

'I'm Cora Blenkinsop. What's all this about?'

Her face became visible through the hair.

Blenkinsop said, 'Get inside, Cora. Finish your tea. You don't have to take any notice of this bleeding copper.'

'If she hasn't done anything wrong, she's nothing to fear from me,' Angel said.

Cora's eyes flashed. 'I *haven't* done anything wrong,' she said. 'But I'd like to know what the policeman wants me for, that's all.'

'If he can't find anything you've done wrong, he'll make summat up, believe me,' Blenkinsop told her. 'Now, Cora, *I am closing this bleeding door.'*

'No, Dad,' Cora said. 'Don't be daft.' She looked up at Angel and said, 'Come in, please. Quickly.'

Blenkinsop grudgingly allowed Angel in and immediately slammed the door shut. 'The house'll be like a bleeding fridge now,' he said. Then he turned round to Cora and said, 'This chap, Angel, is no good, Cora. He was responsible for putting me down for four years and your mother for two, you know. Just be careful what you say. He'll turn what you say into summat discriminating if you're not careful.'

Angel shook his head. 'You know that's not true, Lionel. You were tried fair and square by an independent judge and jury.'

'They were all nobbled,' Blenkinsop said. 'They'd been got at.'

'All thirteen?'

'Every one of them.'

'That doesn't make sense.'

Cora turned to Angel and pointed to the settee. 'Please sit down,' she said as she sat in the easy chair opposite.

'I've warned you, Cora,' Blenkinsop said.

'Aw, buzz off, Dad,' she said. 'Dammit, I'm thirty. I'm old enough to look after myself.'

Blenkinsop shrugged. 'I can do no more,' he said. 'And my tea's going cold.'

He strode angrily out of the front room into the kitchen and banged the door shut.

'Now then, Inspector Angel, what do you want from me?' Cora said.

'I understand that you work for Mr and Mrs Rose at The Brambles, and I wondered if you could help me to understand what is happening there.'

'What do you mean?'

'Well, Mrs Rose believes that the house is haunted by the family who used to live there many years ago, the Cudlipps. Have you seen any evidence of this?'

'Not directly myself, no. But Mrs Rose has seen a few things, and I believe her.'

Angel pursed his lips, then rubbed his chin. 'Is it correct that you have found it impossible to light a fire in that small room near the front door?' he said.

She hesitated.

Angel noticed.

'Yes, it's quite correct,' she said.

'But why? What happens?'

'It won't light. If it does, it goes out almost as soon as you have lit it. I can't explain it. I've tried several times, so has Mrs Rose. Now they are managing with an old two-bar electric fire, but she is not very pleased with the situation.'

'Is there anything else you can tell me about the ghostly activity there?'

'To tell the truth, Inspector, going there don't do my nerves no good. If it gets much worse, I shall have to leave. As it is, I daren't work there when it gets dark.'

'I think I see how it is, Cora,' he said.

'Is there anything I can do to help?'

'You'll be able to answer that better yourself,' he said.

He stood up and made for the door.

Angel was on the phone. It was the sixth garage he had phoned that Wednesday morning. He hoped the sixth call would be lucky.

'Is that Knight's Garage?' he said.

A young lady said yes.

'I understand that you have a gentleman by the name of Paul Rose working there?'

'Yes,' she said. 'He's our reception engineer.'

Ah, bingo!, Angel thought.

'What make of car have you got?' she said.

He had to think quickly. 'BMW,' he said. 'It's an intermittent problem,' he added. 'It doesn't always start straightaway. It's all right most of the time.'

'You'd better bring it in. He could have a look at it. What name is it?'

'Angel,' he said. 'Can I bring it round now?'

'Yes, Mr Angel. Any time,' she said.

'I'll be there in a few minutes.'

He ended the call. Checked on the address. He knew exactly where it was, and he was round there in five minutes. It was only a small business on a busy corner site ideal for petrol and diesel sales. He saw a vacant parking spot in a block of twelve, drove into it, got out and walked past the pumps through a glass door to a 'window' in a pre-fabricated wall that had the word 'Reception' painted over it.

A man in smart blue overalls came up to the window and said, 'Good morning, sir. What can I do for you?'

'Excuse me,' Angel said. 'Are you Paul Rose?'

Rose's eyebrows went up. 'Yes. Have we met before?'

'I don't think so. My name is Angel. I met your wife the other night when—'

'Oh yes. You're a police inspector, aren't you? I want to thank you for all you and your wife did.'

'That's all right, Mr Rose. I didn't do much. I'd like to speak to you for a few minutes. Can you get away?'

He hesitated. His eyes narrowed as he licked his lips, then he said, 'Yes. Of course. I'll just have a word with . . .'

He turned away from the window to speak to somebody unseen by Angel. A moment later he came out of a door near the window, wiping his hands on a piece of oily cloth.

'We can sit in my car,' Angel said.

'I'm all right for five or ten minutes,' Rose said.

They went through the glass door to the BMW.

Rose finished wiping his hands and stuffed the rag in his overall pocket.

'How is Mrs Rose?' Angel said.

'She's fine mostly but she's upset by all the things that are happening in our house.'

'That's what I want to talk to you about. Have you seen any of the ghostly things for yourself?'

'No, to tell the truth I haven't. The whole thing is getting on my nerves. It seems to be monopolizing our lives. All our conversations are about this chap Cudlipp appearing here and there and women disappearing into wardrobes.'

Angel rubbed his chin. 'And what's this about not being able to light a fire in the little room by the front door?'

'Oh, the study? Helen says that whenever she's tried to light a coal fire in there, it goes out.'

'Have you had the chimney swept?'

'Well, no. I hadn't thought of that.'

'It would increase the draught, wouldn't it?'

'Yes, of course,' he said brightly, then his face changed. 'But the cause, according to Cora — she's our daily — is that the paper and sticks are always wet . . . they seem to get wet even though they are bone dry to start with. I don't understand it. Dry paper and sticks don't become wet before your eyes, do they?'

Angel shrugged. 'Have *you* tried to light a fire there?'

'Me? No. Oh no. My wife needs no encouragement. If, for some reason, I couldn't light a fire there, in her mind it would confirm the fact that there are spooks in the house.'

'And you don't believe in spooks, as you call them?'

'I can take them or leave them, Inspector. I worry more about her sanity than I do about spooks. I'm afraid these so-called appearances are really getting to her . . . making her ill. I know it's out of fashion to say that you love your wife, but in my particular case, I do. And I worry about her. She wants a baby desperately. And she's forty. The doctor said that we needed a quiet, peaceful, loving relationship to conceive at her age. When we bought The Brambles, in its own grounds, off the main road, near the woods and with a lovely outlook, we thought we would have all that, but it's not working out that way. If this nonsense continues, we're going to have to sell the house and find somewhere else. And I really don't want to go through all *that* again either.'

Angel sympathized. He hated change, especially when it could easily be avoided.

'Well, give my best wishes to your wife, Mr Rose,' Angel said, 'and I hope things work out right for you both very soon.'

'Thank you, Inspector,' Rose said, 'and thank you for your kind interest.' He climbed out of the car and returned to the garage.

Angel started the car and drove off the garage forecourt, heading for the station. When he had joined the ring road, he began to think. Helen Rose had given such vivid, detailed accounts of what she had seen. To her everything was unmistakably real, but then again, Angel was thinking, dreams *seem* unmistakably real. But was Paul Rose being entirely honest?

He arrived at Bromersley police station and drove the BMW round the back to the station car park and into his parking space.

As he reached his office, his phone began to ring. He picked it up. 'Angel.'

'It's Trevor Crisp, sir.'

Angel's eyes brightened. He was eager to hear his news.

'Yes, lad. What have you got?'

'We're outside Josephine Huxley's house, sir, in the van,' Crisp said. 'There seem to be two people living in the house. Mother and son, I think. We spotted her for the first time yesterday afternoon when she apparently went out shopping.'

'What time did she go out?'

'She went out at 1400 hours on the dot and returned at 16.52, just before her son.'

'Probably back to make a meal for him. What's the son like?'

'Aged twenty to twenty-five. I assume he is her son. He returned yesterday at 17.10, and he went out this morning at 0808 hours, so I expect he has a job.'

'Careful, lad. He might just be going out to shoot pool, collect his money from the Social, call at the bookies and spend the rest of the time in the pub.'

Crisp smiled. 'We'll be careful, sir.'

'What's she look like in real life?'

'Pleasant enough but nothing special, sir. About forty-five, spectacles, dark hair.'

'Not your type, eh?'

He grinned. 'Too old, sir.'

'I've known you chase older.'

'That was when I was too young to know better, sir.'

'Do you know if she has a job at all?'

'Not sure, sir. Doesn't look as if she has.'

'See if that configuration is repeated today, and if it is, consider going in tomorrow afternoon. If she goes out this afternoon, get Scrivens to follow her and find out.'

'I'm more concerned about the man, sir.'

'I understand that, but Ted Scrivens can do both. He can follow her this afternoon and the man tomorrow morning. I would be happier if we knew that the young man was *not* out merely for recreation. I don't want you taking any unnecessary risks.'

'Point taken, sir.'

'Keep me posted.' He returned the phone to its holster.

Angel rubbed his chin really hard. He was asking Crisp to break into a house to set up listening devices, without a warrant. If he was caught, he would be clearly breaking the law, and the householder, in this case Josephine Huxley, who may be totally innocent of any crime, could bring the matter to court. There would be bad publicity for Crisp and Scrivens but mostly for Angel and the force generally. It needed careful planning.

He was ruminating on that theme when there was a knock at the door.

It was Leisha Baverstock. She was carrying a clipboard.

'Come in,' he said.

'Ah, sir,' she said. 'You asked me to check on Vera Malwhinney, Edwin Malwhinney, Hubert Grant and Charles.'

'Yes, Leisha. And did you find anything out?'

'Not from the PNC, sir. There's nothing there on any of them. And I couldn't produce anything anywhere for Charles. You have to have his full name.'

Angel nodded. He was not a bit surprised.

'Anyway, when I inquired at the Inland Revenue about Hubert Grant, HM Revenue and Customs records showed that he was charged at Leeds with an attempt to defraud HM Customs and Excise (as it was known then) of a sum of £22,000 in 1981. He was an on-course bookie at the time, you know. Stood at all the racecourses round here, Doncaster, Lincoln, York, Wetherby, Aintree and so on.'

'Oh, really? So Hubert was a bit of a boy, was he?' Angel said thoughtfully. 'Did he do time?'

'No, sir. He got a hefty fine. Double the amount plus another £20,000 *and* costs.'

'It would be more than a hundred grand. Phew. Right, Leisha. Thank you.'

She went out.

Angel was beginning to think that a pattern was developing. The reason why it was not possible to light a fire in the little room at the front of the house might be because there was something blocking the chimney. He wondered if Paul Rose would take heed of his recommendation to have the chimney swept. He consulted his address book, found the phone number of The Brambles, reached out for the phone and tapped it on to the pad. It was soon answered by Helen Rose, who was very affable.

'I'm fine,' Angel said, 'thank you. I've been making a few inquiries about different aspects of the ghostly things that have been bothering you there, and there is one suggestion I would strongly make. That is to have the chimney swept. In fact, I casually made this suggestion to your husband, Paul, who I saw this morning. In the small room at the front of the house where the fire refuses to be lit, it's possible that the chimney is blocked or partly blocked, which might significantly affect the drawing ability in the grate. That might be why a fire cannot be lit there.'

'Well, we can do that, of course,' Helen Rose said, 'but Cora and I have tried to light fires in that grate several times, and we have noticed that even though we began with dry paper and sticks, they somehow got wet and wouldn't ignite.'

'Well, I don't know if that's because of condensation, but I strongly urge you to call a sweep in.'

'Very well. Inspector Angel, I will. At the earliest opportunity.'

'Good. And I'd like to be present at the time the chimney is swept, if you wouldn't mind?'

'You know you're welcome here any time,' Helen Rose said. 'I'll certainly let you know when I have found a sweep and arranged an appointment.'

TWELVE

DC Ahmed Ahaz was pushing a trolley loaded with letters and packets around the four-storey home of Zenith Television Studios. He was wearing a peak hat with the words *Post Room* embroidered in yellow gilt wire on it and a brown overall with the same words emblazoned in black on the top pocket. Conveniently located in that pocket was his regular police-issue recording machine with a fingertip push-button control so that it could be quickly and easily switched on when needed.

Ahmed's heart thumped a little bit harder at every office he had to enter and every time he had to speak to anybody. He hoped it didn't show. He actually thought he was acting the part quite well and appeared to have been doing the job of post clerk for months rather than hours. He had to make a full tour of all the offices four times a day. Two journeys were to deliver post and two journeys to collect items that had to be posted. He was also called upon to deliver internal post.

He glanced at the Mitto-Amino watch on his wrist and checked the time. It was 11 a.m. He was right on time, if the watch was correct. He was at the beginning of the second journey of the day, delivering the second post, and had just completed deliveries to the top floor, where the chairman and the company directors had their offices. He was now in the lift travelling down to the third floor, where the makers of the programmes, the producers and directors had their offices.

He approached the office of Viktor Berezin and noticed that the door was slightly ajar. He pushed the trolley close to it and could hear voices. Two men were arguing. He switched on the little recording machine in his top pocket.

'You should see a doctor,' the deep foreign voice said. 'You might need to rest.'

'Can't do that,' a lighter voice said. 'No way. There's nobody in the world that could take over my job provided that I keep healthy, available and willing, which I most definitely am. *Nobody.*'

'Don't vorry, Alan. There are at least a dozen presenters out there that could do the job just as well as you, maybe better.'

'Maybe. But you daren't risk any one of them, dare you, Viktor? You're scared the ratings would tumble, and they would.'

Suddenly the alarm on Ahmed's wristwatch began to ring out. His heart came up to his mouth and his face went as red as a judge's cloak. He mustn't get caught on his first solo undercover job! His heart pounded like a Salvation Army drum. His efforts to cancel the buzzing were to no avail, so he snatched up the letters for Berezin, tapped on the open door and went in. 'Excuse me, sir. That's my watch alarm. Sorry but I can't switch it off.'

Both men stared at his very red face, then turned away.

An unhappy Viktor Berezin was seated behind his desk looking as if he had lost a 5p piece through a hole in his pocket, while Alan de Souza was standing at the other side of the desk, one hand in his smart jacket pocket, his nose held high, seemingly smelling the paint on the ceiling.

The alarm stopped and Ahmed feigned a smile.

'Post,' he said, and he quickly put the envelopes in the in-tray on the desk in front of Berezin and said, 'Anything to post, sir?'

'No,' Berezin grunted.

'Thank you, sir,' Ahmed said as he came out. He sighed with relief. He seemed to have got away with it. He was buzzing with excitement. He couldn't wait to find a private corner where he could take out his mobile and transmit the conversation to Angel. He looked at the watch on his wrist. He wished he knew how to operate the alarm.

It was two o'clock and DS Trevor Crisp and DC Edward Scrivens were in the observation van in the leafy suburbs of Birmingham. Scrivens was putting on his raincoat and hat, while Crisp, through the binoculars fitted on a stand in the back of the van, was watching the side door of Josephine Huxley's semi-detached house.

After a few minutes, the door opened and Mrs Huxley came out carrying a plastic shopping bag.

'She's on her way,' Crisp said. 'Wearing that same bottle-green coat with the fur trim.'

He leaned over, switched on the video camera and returned to the binoculars.

'She's no taste,' Crisp added. 'She may have stacks of money, but she's no taste.'

Scrivens, having pulled on his leather gloves, was standing with his hand on the back door handle of the van.

'I'm ready, Sarge,' Scrivens said.

'She's come through the gate and turned *left*, the same as yesterday,' Crisp said. 'A creature of habit, I am happy to say. Good luck.'

'I'm off,' Scrivens said and he opened the van door.

He had to walk fast at first to get her in his sights. There weren't many cars and practically no pedestrians on that gloomy November afternoon.

Eventually he caught sight of her at the opposite side of the street, carrying the plastic shopping bag, which looked quite heavy.

She walked pretty fast and Scrivens had to be watchful to maintain a sensible distance behind her.

She turned left at the end of the street on to a wider road comprising larger houses. Trees were planted every twenty yards or so along it. It led to a shopping precinct of about eight shops. Mrs Huxley stopped momentarily to look in the newsagent's window. Scrivens also stopped and positioned himself behind a convenient tree, just in case she looked back.

After a few seconds he edged forward to see her but she had gone. Disappeared. He gasped. He mustn't lose her. His pulse was racing. It was absolutely vital that he found out how Mrs Huxley occupied her time in the afternoon. He crossed the road, his eyes scanning the shopping precinct like an auctioneer looking for a bidder. He went in each shop in turn and she didn't appear to be in any of them. Next to the butcher's at the end was a building with a sign that said 'Council Offices'. He went in. He saw signs that said 'Clinic', 'Council Tax' and 'Library'. He tried the clinic door. It led to a room with chairs on all sides like a waiting room. A young woman was busy knitting something in white. There was a tiny reception window. A girl saw him and she peered through it.

She giggled and said, 'Can I help you?'

Scrivens licked his lips. He didn't know what to say. 'What's that?' he said.

'Did you want somebody?'

'Is this where I see the doctor?' he said.

'You can't see the doctor here this afternoon,' she replied, still smiling. 'This is the women's clinic.'

Scrivens didn't care what was happening. He only wanted to know if Josephine Huxley was in any of those rooms beyond. But he couldn't come straight out with it.

The door opened behind him and a young woman who was obviously heavily pregnant came in. He looked back at the lady who was knitting and realized that she also was expecting a happy event . . . It began to dawn on him where he was. His face coloured up. He now knew why the girl was laughing at him. It also occurred to him that Josephine Huxley was not likely to be there at her age.

He made for the door. 'Right . . . erm, thank you,' he said, and closed the door quickly.

He tried the door handle to the council tax office but it wouldn't open. It was obviously locked. He turned and saw the double swing-doors to the library. He pushed one of the doors and went in, heading to the reception desk. His heart was thumping. He knew DS Crisp would be dismayed if he lost Josephine Huxley, and DI Angel wouldn't be pleased.

'Can I help you?' the woman at the reception desk said.

Scrivens turned round sharply. 'Oh yes,' he said. 'I was looking for a book.'

'Oh yes? What's the title of it?'

'I can't quite remember,' he said.

'Well,' she said, 'what's the author's name?'

'Do you know, I've forgotten that as well.'

'Well, what's it about?'

'Erm . . . it's about two men.'

'Two men? Is that all? Aren't there any women in it?'

'Oh yes. There are two women in it as well.'

'Two men and two women?'

'Erm, yes. And a dog. If I could just come in and take a look round the shelves it might come back to me.'

'Can I see your library ticket, please?'

'Library ticket. Library ticket? Oh yes.' He made a show of looking through his pockets, then he said, 'Sorry. I'm afraid I've forgotten it.'

The librarian leaned forward and in a quiet voice said, 'Are you registered with the library?'

As she leaned forward, Scrivens was able to see behind her through an open door of a room marked 'Reference Library', and he saw a woman sitting at a long table with a pile of books in front of her, and her nose in another one. She was wearing a green coat with a fur collar. It was Josephine Huxley. Joy upon joy! He was so relieved. He sighed silently. He lowered his shoulders and smiled.

The librarian's patience was wearing thin. 'I said *are you registered with the central library*?'

'I am so sorry,' he said. He was trying to think fast. 'I'm not sure about that. Do you know, I think I will leave it. Sorry to have been a trouble to you. Good afternoon.'

He left swiftly.

The librarian almost boiled over. There was a pile of returned books in front of her. She cooled herself down by checking them off and banging each of them in turn loudly on the counter top.

Out in the cold, he took up a position across the road behind the trunk of a tree. He expected a long wait. He knew that yesterday she had arrived at her home at 16.52 and, as she lived a ten-minute walk away, she may not come out of the library until 16.42. That meant he may have to wait more than two hours.

It was five o'clock and Angel was in his office on the phone to Scrivens, who was reporting on his observation of Mrs Josephine Huxley.

'So I had to wait a good two hours, sir,' Scrivens said. 'She came out of the library at 16.35 hours and I followed her back home, where DS Crisp spotted her — although it was dark — arriving at 16.45.'

'Well, I expect she was swotting up for the programme next Sunday night, lad. There doesn't seem to be anything terrible about that. Put me back on to DS Crisp.'

Scrivens handed the phone to the sergeant.

'Now then, Trevor, I don't want you to take any unnecessary risks tomorrow. If the circumstances are not right, you'll have to wait until they are.'

Crisp said, 'Well, sir, she got back at almost the same time as the day before, which, if she does the same again tomorrow, will give me a window of two and three-quarters of an hour. I only need ten minutes max. That's easy-peasy.'

Angel sighed. 'I hope you're right, lad. Of course you have still to check out what the son is up to.'

'Yes, sir. We're geared up for that first thing tomorrow morning.'

'Right, Trevor. Speak to you later.'

He replaced the phone in its holster and reached out for his coat.

It was ten minutes past eight on Thursday when Tom Huxley came out of the side door of his home into the early-morning November mist and dark clouds.

DS Crisp was already in the observation van looking through the binoculars at the house.

'Off you go, Ted,' Crisp said. 'He's going in the same direction as he went yesterday.'

'Right, Sarge,' Scrivens said as he opened the van door. He got out and closed the door quietly.

Scrivens soon picked him out in the quiet street. He followed him, carefully keeping sixty yards or so behind him on the opposite side of the road. He had no idea where the young man was headed, but as he had left home at about that time the previous morning, it was assumed that he was headed for a place of regular employment.

Huxley maintained a steady pace through the outskirts of the city for around fifteen minutes, making several turns but in the same general direction. There were a few cars with their sidelights on travelling up and down the gloomy streets and a few pedestrians.

After turning yet another corner, Scrivens saw the bright lights of a small shopping frontage, where he eventually recognized an illuminated sign indicating a branch of Cheapo's Handy Market and the illuminated windows of a newsagent's, a hairdressing salon, a chemist, a bank and an independent butcher's.

Scrivens increased his pace so that he did not miss any quick turns Huxley might make if his destination was to be any of the shops. He watched Huxley walk across the front of all the shops and then disappear down a small alleyway at the end.

Scrivens sped up to the alley and looked down it. There was a door at the end. It was a side door into Cheapo's. He checked his watch. It was twenty-five past eight. Huxley's shift must start at 8.30. He noticed the store trolleys outside on the pavement and saw several customers wandering round the aisles. He realized the store was already open and must have been open for some time. He drifted out of the bright lights into the mist and relative gloom of the opposite side of the road, where he could still observe the side door. He remained there for ten minutes then strode boldly across the road, went into Cheapo's and picked up a wire basket near the door. He sauntered down the aisles trying to look interested in the posters, the groceries, the prices and the special offers. It was some minutes before he saw double doors burst open at the far end of the store and a trolley six feet high loaded with chocolate Father Christmases being pushed along an aisle into the store. A young man in the white and red livery of the store was pushing it from behind. As he passed by, Scrivens was pleased to see that it was Tom Huxley.

It was ten o'clock when Mr Goode of the All Electric Sweep Company pulled up his three-wheeler van outside The Brambles.

He knocked on the door and was admitted by Cora Blenkinsop and shown into the little room at the front of the house.

DI Angel had arrived five minutes earlier and was standing amidst acres of dust sheets covering all the furniture and most of the carpet. He was drinking coffee with Helen Rose.

Goode looked at Angel and nodded, then looked at Helen Rose and said, 'This the chimney you want sweeping, missus?'

'Yes, please,' Helen Rose said.

He took a look at the fireplace, nodded and said, 'Hmm. That's an old one but not to worry. This is the All Electric Sweep Company. It won't take me long and there'll be no mess. You'll want to see the brush out of the chimney top, I 'spect?'

'I do,' Helen Rose said.

'No problem. I'll tell you when I'm through.'

He went out to his van and in two trips he brought in bags of brushes, extensions, a vacuum cylinder, a knee pad, a roll of electric cable, and a wide roll of sticky tape.

Ten minutes later, he had a thick fabric stuck on the black bricks round the mouth of the chimney with sticky tape. Through a small hole in the middle of the fabric was the brush and the vacuum pipe head, and he was beginning the process of screwing an extension piece to the brush handle. He had only screwed one extension to the brush when he found that the brush head had come up against something immoveable. He tried all ways to make headway but to no avail. The object in the chimney, whatever it was, couldn't be moved.

'Oh,' he said, pulling a disappointed face. He switched off the vacuum and looked up at Angel. 'There's something up there that the brush can't get round, sir.'

Angel's eyebrows shot up. 'Oh yes?' he said. He came closer to the fireplace.

'Can I do anything, Mr Goode?' Helen Rose said.

'No, ma'am. It's all right. Just a minute. I have to get something from the van.'

Two minutes later Goode returned with a rod around six feet long. At one end were two rows of teeth that had a grabbing action operated by rotating the handle at the bottom. He soon had the brush disconnected and the grabber through the opening in the fabric in its place. He switched on the vacuum and attempted to reach up to the obstruction.

'It seems soft,' he said. 'Oh dear . . . I can't get a grip . . . it slips through . . . oh dear . . . ah! Yes, I think I've got it . . . yes, I have.' He locked the grabber at the end and began to pull hard. His forehead showed lines of perspiration loaded with soot.

Angel watched him. He thought it must be something substantial.

'There is something there then, Inspector,' said Helen.

Goode was pulling hard and then it suddenly gave way. There was the sound of something relatively soft falling in the grate.

The fabric round the grate billowed out and the sucking noise of the vacuum increased to a high-pitched scream.

Goode turned it off. The silence was welcome.

He looked up at Helen Rose. 'Whatever it is, I'll now be able to sweep your chimney. I can tell from the sound of the vacuum.'

Angel came across and said, 'Let's see what you've brought down.'

Goode took the end of the sticky tape and peeled it from the bricks round the fireplace, taking the fabric with it.

Angel squatted down to see but it was a bit difficult because whatever it was covered in soot. Goode's fingers were all over it. It seemed to be a coat of some sort wrapped round something heavier. 'Leave that there, lad,' Angel suddenly said. 'Don't touch them anymore, Mr Goode. I want to take these items to be examined forensically. Won't be a minute.'

Angel rushed off to his car and returned with a brown paper sack with the word *EVIDENCE* printed in red on each side.

'Put that bundle in there, please, Mr Goode,' he said.

The sweep put the black soot-covered bundle in the sack. 'There you are, sir. I don't know what use that will be to you, but good luck to it, I say.'

Then he looked in the fireplace grate. There was a small layer of soot, but nothing else.

Goode took a torch out of his pocket and shone it up the chimney. He reached up and looked at it from all angles. At length he said, 'Well, there's no gap, no marks, no damage or nothing. Some people think that it's all right to stuff anything up a chimney . . . I don't know . . . Chimneys is not rubbish dumps. There's nothing more nice than a clean chimney. That's what I say.'

He re-stuck the sticky tape on the black-painted bricks around the fire grate, switched on the vacuum and continued with the sweeping operation.

After a few minutes, Angel turned to Mrs Rose. 'Everything seems straightforward now,' he said. 'I'll be on my way to get this stuff looked at by forensics.'

She nodded and smiled at him. 'Do you mind seeing yourself out?' she said.

'Not at all,' he said. He picked up the brown paper sack and made for the door.

THIRTEEN

DS Trevor Crisp and DC Edward Scrivens were in the observation van in the leafy suburbs of Birmingham. Scrivens was loading the video machine with new tape, and Crisp was looking through the binoculars at the side door of Josephine Huxley's house while tapping a loud and regular beat on the bench top with his free hand.

'Come on. Come on,' Crisp said. 'It's two o'clock. Where is she? Come on. Come on. Damn it. It's time she was off to that library.'

'I don't suppose you *have* to do it, Sarge, do you?' Scrivens said.

'No, I don't,' Crisp said. 'In fact if Angel told me I had to, I wouldn't. And he couldn't do a thing about it.'

Scrivens nodded thoughtfully. 'I suppose I would do the same as you, if I was in your shoes.'

'Well, why not?' Crisp said. 'Look, we've cased the joint for two days. I *know* there are only two people living there. I know where *she* goes and for how long, and that the son works at Cheapo's and finishes at five, so he couldn't get back here before ten past five at the earliest. And I know it's an easy lock cos I've had a look at it close up. It's easy-peasy. Couldn't be easier.'

Scrivens nodded.

'What is the exact time?' Crisp said.

Scrivens looked at his wrist. 'Two o'clock on the button.'

'That's what I've got. *Where* is she? Now that I'm all geared up for it, looks like Josephine Huxley is changing her plans. That's the trouble with women, Ted. You can *learn* from this.'

'Learn what?'

Crisp didn't hear him. 'Do you know what, the lenses on these binoculars are all steamed up,' he said. 'Have you got a cloth?'

'A cloth?' Scrivens said. 'There's one in the cab.'

Crisp reached into his trouser pocket and pulled out a handkerchief. 'Never mind, I'll use this.'

He gave each lens a quick wipe, shoved the handkerchief back into his pocket and returned to concentrating on Josephine Huxley's house.

'I reckon I've spent at least half my life waiting for women. Do you know that, Ted?'

Scrivens had completed aligning the direction of the lens on the video recorder and began to watch the side door of Huxley's through a smaller pair of binoculars.

'No, never,' Scrivens said with a grin.

'It's true. For a start, the first nine months of my life I spent waiting on my mother, didn't I? Then as an infant I was always waiting to be changed or bathed or fed or something, always by a woman. At school we had to wait in line for everything, roll call, books, school dinners, almost always for a teacher or a playground supervisor, who were almost always women. And if I ask a girl out, she might be on time the *first* time, but when she thinks she's got you, thereafter you have to wait. So how long do you think you'd have to wait if you were *married* to one?'

'Is *that* why you're not married, Sarge?'

'Naw. The point is that now, even in this job, at thirty-two years of age, I am *still* waiting for a woman.'

Scrivens suddenly lowered the binoculars, switched on the video recorder and said, 'You don't have to wait any longer, Sarge. She's coming out now.'

Crisp's eyebrows shot up. 'I see her,' Crisp said. 'Aaaah. At last.' He continued watching her. He wanted to check that she was carrying the carrier bag that he believed was filled with books, which she was, and that she was intent on turning in the direction of the library, which she did.

Crisp looked up from the binocular stand at Scrivens. 'Right, Ted. I'm going in right away,' he said as he reached out for his raincoat. 'I have all I need in my pockets. I only need about five minutes in the house. I'll phone you on the house phone to test it and for you to get the number. In the unlikely event of anyone approaching the house, ring me on my mobile. OK?'

'OK, Sarge, good luck.'

Crisp buttoned his coat, pulled on his gloves, got out of the van, crossed the road and walked up the street towards Mrs Huxley's house.

Scrivens took up the position behind the binoculars in the back of the observation van and carefully watched Crisp's progress.

Crisp reached the front gate, opened it and went through it. He went straight up to the side door and rang the bell. He waited a respectable few moments then, resisting the temptation of looking round, he pulled out of his pocket a thin piece of sheet plastic about eight inches long by one inch wide. He entered it between the door and the door jamb by the lock, gave it a sharp tap with a closed fist and the latch slipped back. He then turned the knob and pushed at the door and it opened. His heart began to pump hard as he went inside. He didn't waste a moment. He found the telephone. It was in the hall on an occasional table. It was staring at him as soon as he opened the door. He dug into his pocket for a small box and took out a miniature transmitter and from a pad pulled off a small piece of Blu-Tack. He unscrewed the earpiece cover of the telephone, tucked a tiny transmitter into the cavity then screwed the cover back on. Then he dialled Scrivens' mobile.

It was answered on the first ring. 'Yes, Sarge?'

'Everything OK. Record this phone's number, Ted.'

'Right, Sarge. Be careful.'

Crisp smiled and quickly replaced the phone. He had a quick glance at the downstairs accommodation. In the room at the back of the house he saw a big slimline TV, two comfortable easy chairs and a sofa. There were three books open on the floor at the side of one of the chairs. Squeezed in the corner was a small table on which there were piles of more books and newspapers, and a computer keyboard, screen and tower. He decided that that was the room Josephine and Tom Huxley were likely to occupy more than any of the others. He rolled a small piece of Blu-Tack round a second transmitter, borrowed a chair from the kitchen and stuck it on the top side of a small chandelier that was suspended from the middle of the ceiling. He had just returned the chair to the kitchen when his mobile rang out.

The shrill noise made him gasp and breathe more quickly. He looked at the LCD on the phone and it told him it was Scrivens calling. 'Yes?' he said.

'Josephine Huxley is on her way up the garden path.'

Crisp gasped. The sound of his increased heartbeat thrashed in his ears. He closed the phone. He heard a key enter the lock. He dashed out of the kitchen to the sitting room and stood behind the door.

He heard her open the side door and come into the hall.

He peered at her through the crack between the door and the door jamb. She was carrying several bags of shopping. She went into the kitchen and heaved them on to the table. He heard her fill a kettle and the click of a switch. Then he heard light music, presumably from a transistor radio. She began to put the shopping away. She looked as if she had come to stay. He wondered how on earth he was going to get out of the house before she saw him. If Angel knew about this, he would probably kill him.

Meanwhile Scrivens' heart was thumping. He was wondering what he could do to get DS Crisp out of this mess. He couldn't just sit there looking at the house through binoculars. He sighed and hurriedly reached out for his coat. He locked the van then legged it across the road and up the street to the house. His mouth was dry. He had never been in a predicament like this before. He had no idea what he was going to say or do.

Mrs Huxley had made herself a hot drink and was finishing tidying up the kitchen. She took some books out of a bag and looked at the titles. She advanced towards Crisp. He saw her through the slit. He held his breath. He darted away from the back of the door to the floor behind the settee. She came through the hall into the sitting room and put the books on the table where the computer was. Then she saw the books on the floor. She picked them up, closed them and put them on the table. Crisp's heart was pounding. She left the room.

As she arrived in the hall on her way to the kitchen, the doorbell rang. 'Oh dear,' she said. She turned back and opened the door.

It was Ted Scrivens.

She looked him up and down.

He remembered a trick played on householders by villains to rob them. He hoped it might work equally well to get Crisp out of the house.

Scrivens said, 'I was just passing and I noticed your chimney pot. I am a builder, you see. I thought I should tell you about it before it does you any damage.'

Mrs Huxley frowned and put her hand to her chin. 'Oh,' she said. 'What's the matter with it?'

'Well, it's not safe. You need to *see* it,' he said, edging away from the door and hoping she would follow him. 'I'll show you, if you follow me.'

She came down the step and followed him up the path, through the front gate on to the pavement.

'You can see it from here best,' he said.

He edged up the road a little so that she was just out of vision of her side door but he could still plainly see it. 'We need to be about here.'

He looked up at the roof of her house and said, 'Now, you see that chimney pot on your house? The one on the left? It's sloping.'

She looked up, frowned and was very uncertain. 'Yes,' she said.

'Well, in the wind, it rocks because it has no cement holding it. The years and weather have weakened it and worn it all away. One day, when it is really windy, it will blow off and possibly crash through your tiles into the house causing untold damage, or it might roll down the tiles and crash on to somebody below.'

Out of the corner of his eye, he saw Crisp come out of Mrs Huxley's door and dash down the back yard and out of her back gate. Thank God for that, he thought. He sighed. He turned back to the woman.

She still had her hand to her face. 'Well, what do I ought to do?'

'Tell your husband. He needs to get a builder go round your chimney pots with some cement and see that they're safe. That's all.'

Mrs Huxley looked up at the roof again. 'Which chimney pot did you say is unsafe?'

He looked up at the roof of the house and said, 'I thought it was the one on the left. Actually, it doesn't look too bad from here now. You might get through this winter all right. Anyway, I must be off.'

'Well, thank you, young man,' she said. 'Thank you very much.'

'Not at all. Good afternoon.'

She frowned and shook her head as she walked back down her garden path.

Scrivens moved quickly up the road away from the scene. He was thinking that Crisp would get back to the observation van before him and he hadn't a key.

Angel was at his desk reading a small booklet headed 'New guidance for entering all households'. It was issued by

ACPO's National Community Tension Team. Angel found it very boring. It related to all race and faith communities and applied chiefly to police personnel involved in counter terrorism operations. It was at pains to point out that it was a counter terrorism unit of MI5 that quelled a prison riot involving prisoners taking two officers as hostages at York prison earlier that year. It was the sort of thing every policeman was obligated to read and observe.

There was a knock on the door.

'Come in,' he said.

He looked up. It was DS Taylor clutching an A4 sheet of paper.

'What you got, Don?'

'That stuff you took out of that chimney, sir . . . it was a long brown linen coat, a sort of overall, the kind that warehousemen used to wear thirty years ago. And wrapped inside it was a pair of old shoes. They had been good quality all-leather shoes, but they were very worn and burned in places.'

'Well, they did come from a chimney.'

'Oh no, sir. They weren't burned from being up the chimney. They were burned, I suspect, from molten gold.'

'Molten gold?'

'Yes. As it's being poured it sometimes spits out a spot or two that lands still molten and makes odd shapes wherever it cools. And there are minute traces in the soles of the shoes and gold dust in the pockets of the coat.'

Angel sat back in the swivel chair. 'Somebody been melting gold down to reform it into something else?'

'If they weren't making it into jewellery, then it was possibly being formed into ingots and sold to bullion dealers.'

'Yes but why stuff the coat and shoes up there?'

'Was it to hide them to conceal the fact that a home furnace was in operation here, or simply to bung up the chimney so that a fire couldn't be lit?'

'A bunged-up chimney wouldn't cause the sticks and paper to be wet, would it?'

'Don't see that it would, sir.'

‘Hmm. How long do you think the coat and shoes have been there, Don?’

‘It’s very hard to say, sir. I could only guess at sometime between say two years and twenty years. I could be wrong.’

‘Sounds reasonable, lad. Whichever it is, it would put it in the time of the previous owner of the house, Hubert Price. He was the owner of Aladdin’s Cave on Market Street. It was a sort of antique and curio shop. His slogan was “I buy owt”. I bet he bought plenty of gold over the years — stolen or bought honestly. He used to have a sign up, I remember. I bet those shoes and coat belonged to him. Is there any way we can check on that, Don?’

‘Not unless we had his DNA and I could find a hair or a spot of dried blood on the coat to compare. I might be able — with a lot of luck — to find a hair on the coat but I doubt we could get any DNA from him without digging him up.’

‘And he was probably cremated. Anyway, if we could prove it, we couldn’t bring anything against him now.’

‘Do you want me to do any more work on these items, sir?’

‘No. I think it’s a safe bet to assume the coat and shoes were his. Put them somewhere safe for the time being. They may be needed as evidence. Thank you, Don.’

‘Right, sir,’ Taylor said.

It was three o’clock on Thursday afternoon, 21 November, and DC Ahmed Ahaz was on his rounds as post clerk in Studio Two at Zenith Television. It was unusually quiet because the studio was not in use at that time.

From the working lights up in the gods, he was navigating his trolley between furniture, scenery, back projection screens, props, banks of lighting and technical equipment. It was his last tour delivering and collecting letters and packets for that day. He was heading for the three small offices at the far side of the floor when suddenly he heard somebody say, ‘You said I’d be amply rewarded, but I haven’t been.’

He stopped and listened. It was coming from the other side of a set of flats. It was a man but he couldn't identify him.

A man with a foreign voice replied: 'I said I vud *try* and see that you would be amply rewarded.'

Ahmed's eyebrows went up. It was the unmistakable voice of Viktor Berezin. He switched on the recording machine in his top pocket and listened.

'You said that you'd find me a director's job in the States or even Australia,' the unknown man said.

'Nonsense,' Berezin said. 'I said I'd find you a job there if it all went wrong here and you got ze sack, which it hasn't. It hasn't been exposed yet and I am hopeful it will not have to be. But you haven't earned your wheat. I am not paying you for work not done. You said you vud find out how the money tree works. But you haven't told me anysing I didn't already know.'

'I told you *who* makes it work?'

'Zat's not new. I already knew zat. It's the mechanics of the thing, the details but also ze proof. I must have ze proof. So that we can get him by the short and curlies.'

'How can I possibly get proof? He's far too crafty.'

At that point, a door nearby opened and then closed.

'Somebody's coming,' the voice said.

Ahmed heard two sets of footsteps walking away in opposite directions. He switched off the recorder and returned to pushing the trolley towards the offices. He looked round to see if he could see discover the owner of the voice. He didn't see either man.

He finished his round and returned to the post room.

His boss was waiting for him. 'Tha's been a long time, Ahmed. Now, look, lad. Check off the size and weight of all the stuff to be despatched. Enter it in the book. Then frank it and put it in that bag for collection by the post van by four o'clock. You'll have to be quick. I've got to go out. The chairman wants to see me.'

Ahmed knew that to mean he was going out for a crafty smoke on the fire escape. He reckoned he would just have time to phone Angel and play the recording to him.

'Great stuff, Ahmed,' Angel said from his desk at the station. 'It's a pity you weren't able to find the identity of the man *with* Berezin. It sounds like he's the very man we are looking for.'

Ahmed's eyes flashed. 'You mean he's the murderer, sir?'

'One of them over there is,' Angel said. 'Carry on and keep in touch.'

'Right, sir.'

FOURTEEN

It was 3.45 p.m. on Thursday, 21 November.

Angel picked up the phone and tapped in a number.

A young woman answered. 'Ackroyd and Whitehouse, estate agents and auctioneers. Rachel speaking, can I help you?'

'I want to speak to Archie Ackroyd, please. This is Michael Angel.'

'Thank you. Putting you through.'

'Hello, Michael, what can I do for you?'

'I want you to do me a small favour, Archie. I want you to act as estate agents for a recent client of yours, Paul and Helen Rose.'

'Oh yes. If I can, I will,' Ackroyd said. Then he added, 'Don't tell me they want to sell The Brambles so soon?'

'I'm afraid they do. And they want *you* to offer it for sale. After all, you know all about it, don't you? But she wants . . . well, actually, it's me. *I* want you to offer it for sale at no charge.'

'No charge? Why, is it for charity or something?'

'No. It's not a charity.'

'Well, it's a beautiful house, with great views over the west and south sides, but they might not get back what they paid for it. Why are they selling it?'

'What I want you to do is advertise it in the *Bromersley Chronicle* in exactly the same way you would do in usual circumstances. You will be fully reimbursed for the cost of that, of course. And you won't be out of pocket. It's just your time and expertise I want for free.'

'*Then* what do you want me to do?'

'Get started with that, Archie, will you? Look at the time. I'll have a word with you later about everything else. I have to catch a young lady as she leaves work. Goodbye.'

Ten minutes later, Angel stopped the BMW at the side of the road on Havercroft Lane, just out of sight of The Brambles' front gate. He switched off the ignition and waited.

In the gloomy light, through his car rear mirror he watched the pavement and just after four o'clock he saw a woman come into view. He quickly got out of the car and went up to her.

'Hello, Cora,' he said.

She stared up at him curiously.

'It's Inspector Angel, Bromersley police,' he said.

'Oh, I *know* who you are,' Cora Blenkinsop said. 'I just wondered what you want?'

'Are you going home? I can give you a lift,' he said. 'We can talk as we go.'

She shrugged. 'If you like,' she said.

He opened the nearside car door. She got in. He closed the door and went round to the other side.

When he had started the engine, put on the lights and pulled away from the kerb, he said, 'Has Mrs Rose told you that she and her husband have decided to sell The Brambles?'

'Yes,' she said. 'She told me just before I came out. That'll put me out of work.'

'Sorry about that, Cora. I suppose it will,' he said as he changed up to top gear. 'If I hear of anybody wanting help in the house, I'll let you know.'

She nodded. 'Right, Inspector. Thank you.'

'It's good that you are keeping out of trouble, Cora, isn't it?' he said.

She stared at him in surprise. 'I've never been in trouble,' she said.

'When both your mum and dad have served time in prison,' he said, 'as has happened in your case, it often doesn't serve as a warning to the next generation. Instead the children seem to think it is a licence for them to copy their parents and also behave dishonestly, so that many a time the children finish up serving time too. That's tragic, isn't it? And ridiculous.'

He stopped at some traffic lights and waited patiently for them to change to green. He turned on to the ring road. 'Did your mother tell you what it was like in Holloway?'

Eventually she said, 'Well, she certainly didn't . . . like it.'

'It's pretty awful, Cora, I can tell you. I've had a look round it. The cells are still the original cells. And the petty restrictions are extremely hard to bear. Practically every little thing has to be earned. I don't mean by work, I mean by behaviour. You have to earn the privilege of having a pillow, of using the phone, or of having a transistor in your cell. I don't know how the inmates stand it. And do you know most of the women are in jail because of some blind allegiance to some man who often has pretended to love them or has promised them a gold palace or something? But it's usually pie in the sky. Once the man has got the money or the sex or whatever it is, he will dump her for some classier, richer, more beautiful woman, and then chase after an even bigger trophy.'

She frowned. 'Are you trying to tell me something, Inspector?' Cora said.

Angel pursed his lips. 'No. Just shop talk.'

He turned into Canal Road. 'But if there's anything you want to tell me, this would be a good opportunity, before we get to your house.'

She shook her head.

A few moments later, he stopped the car outside number 102. 'Here we are,' Angel said.

Cora Blenkinsop didn't say a word. She quickly got out, closed the car door, rushed across the pavement and let herself into the house.

Angel watched the door close. He wrinkled his nose, let in the clutch and immediately drove the BMW back to The Brambles. He had an arrangement with Helen Rose and DS Taylor to meet there at a quarter past four.

He saw that Taylor had already arrived because the white SOCO van was at the top of drive. He pulled the BMW behind it. He switched off the lights and the engine and went up to the back door.

Mrs Rose admitted him. 'Good afternoon, Inspector,' she said.

'Good afternoon, Mrs Rose,' he said. 'You'll be pleased to know that everything is all set. The ad for the sale of The Brambles should be in the *Bromersley Chronicle* tomorrow.'

She smiled. 'Thank you. I hope the plan works, Inspector.'

'It'll work, Mrs Rose. Just you see.'

She nodded. 'Your sergeant is in the sitting room. Please follow me.'

'I've only just arrived, sir,' Taylor said.

Angel nodded then turned to Mrs Rose and said, 'Please show us the room where you believe you saw a woman's dress disappear into your wardrobe.'

'Of course. Please follow me,' she said. She switched on the hall and landing lights.

The two men followed. Taylor carried a large bag on a sling on his shoulder.

She led the way upstairs into the front bedroom, switched on the light and pointed to a handsome old mahogany wardrobe.

Angel looked at it and said, 'It's built-in, isn't it? It must have been here when you bought the house.'

'It was indeed, Inspector,' she said.

He turned to Taylor and said, 'Take a look at it, Don. See what you can find.'

Taylor put down his bag, unzipped it and pulled out a hammer with a rubber head. He opened the wardrobe door and was faced with lots of clothes: women's dresses and men's suits and coats.

Helen Rose stepped forward. 'I'm sorry. I should have thought of that. I'll take those out. You understand I don't come up here on my own after dark.' She reached inside and began to lift out bunches of coat hangers with garments suspended from them. Angel stepped forward and assisted her. They put them all on the bed. Then Taylor climbed into the wardrobe. There was ample room for him in there except for the height. He was about eight inches too tall to be able to stand upright. He began a gentle tapping operation with his hammer.

Angel and Mrs Rose stood by waiting, watching and listening.

After a few minutes of gentle tapping, Taylor came out of the wardrobe. 'I've defined a big area that echoes,' he said with a smile.

Angel looked at Mrs Rose and smiled. Out of politeness, she smiled back.

Taylor went over to his bag. He found a stick of chalk and a measuring tape, then climbed back into the wardrobe. Quite soon he looked out of the wardrobe door and said, 'There's an area in the centre at the back that is five foot four by two foot six. Now the difficult part: finding how to get into it.'

'Anything I can do?' Angel said.

Taylor pointed to his bag. 'There's a torch and a big magnet in there, sir.'

Angel found them and passed them up to him.

Taylor turned back into the wardrobe. Minutes later, there was a click, followed by the creaking of dry timber and then the squeal of hinges that had never seen oil.

Angel looked at Mrs Rose, who looked surprised.

A few seconds later Taylor turned round to face them. 'You open it by sliding the middle hook to the left. It's a space cut into the stonework. It's big enough for a man or a woman to hide in. They wouldn't be able to move around much. Probably used by Amos Cudlipp to hide his fancy women.'

'Is there anything in there, Don?'

'Just a minute,' he said. He turned round and fumbled about a little while then came out with a black great-coat, a stovepipe top hat and a white silk woman's underskirt.

When Mrs Rose saw them, she gasped and turned away.

Angel looked at them, rubbed his chin, looked at her and said, 'Hmm. The big coat and the hat would explain the appearance that evening outside the slaughterhouse, wouldn't they?'

Helen Rose could only nod.

Angel said, 'And the silk skirt would explain what you saw disappearing into the wardrobe, wouldn't it?' He didn't wait for a reply. He turned to Taylor. 'Bag those items, Don. Let's hope we find confirmatory forensic on each of them.'

He turned back to Helen Rose.

'Now we need to know why you have never been able to light a fire in the study downstairs.'

She nodded.

'Come on,' he said. 'We can tidy this up later. Let's go and have a look at that fireplace.'

The three of them trundled downstairs, Taylor bringing up the rear with his bag on his shoulder.

Angel moved the electric fire out of the way and, peering at the mass of black-painted bricks that formed the grate, took out his penknife and scratched a tiny flake of paint off one of the bricks. Underneath it reflected a shiny yellow colour.

He turned and looked at Taylor. They nodded and smiled.

Then Angel said, 'Have you brought the nitric acid?'

Taylor quickly dived into his bag and produced a small brown bottle with a white screw cap. Angel carefully unscrewed the cap and with the glass rod sticking out of the screw cap, he transferred a tiny drop of the nitric acid on to the yellow scratch on the brick. It began to bubble ferociously. He wiped the area clean with a white tissue and looked at it. It was bright yellow.

He smiled and showed it to Taylor.

'Twenty-four carat, sir,' he said.

Angel nodded and turned to Mrs Rose. 'Looks like you're a very wealthy woman. If all the bricks under the black paint are gold, you're a multi-millionaire. How does it feel?'

Mrs Rose just stood there, open mouthed.

Taylor said, 'I'll go and finish off upstairs, sir.'

'Right, Don,' Angel said.

Helen Rose then said, 'But, Inspector, how did you know?'

'I didn't. Just put two and two together. Finding the overalls bunging up the chimney. Gold dust in the pockets. Ghosts appearing and disappearing. But not known to have ever appeared *before* you bought the house. A home help who isn't honest. It all came together. Made the impossible possible. Somebody wanted you out of the house.'

'But . . . but . . . Who is the owner of the gold?'

'As far as I know, you are. You are the owner of the freehold of the house, aren't you?'

'Yes. But how did it get there?'

'I suspect the previous owner of the house hid it there, the late Hubert Grant. A lifetime's saving from cash deals as a bookie and then buying old gold at his shop in the town. He was melting it down into moulds then building a fireplace with them and painting it black. Safest place in the world, provided you don't want to light a fire.'

Helen Rose came up close to Angel. 'I'll always be grateful to you, Inspector. I honestly thought I was going crazy.'

'Not you, Mrs Rose. Not you.'

'What do you want me to do now?'

'Nothing. Just sit tight. Leave it to us.'

It was six o'clock on Thursday evening, 21 November. Crisp and Scrivens were at the bench in the observation van watching the big reel of recording tape rotating slowly. They were both wearing earphones and listening in to the conversation between Josephine Huxley and her son, Tom.

They had already overheard an hour of chatter that was in no way incriminating and they were wondering if the entire evening promised to be so uneventful.

After a few moments of silence, they heard the rustle of paper, then Tom Huxley said, 'I'd love a yacht like that, Mum. Look.'

'I might be able to afford to buy you a rowing boat,' she said with a laugh.

There was a pause and then Tom Huxley said, 'You know when you get up to a million, what happens then?'

'What do you mean? There's no certainty he'll let me get *that* far.'

'I thought the deal was that there was no limit.'

'Well, that's what he *said*.'

There was a pause followed by the rattle of pots and cutlery.

'Provided the viewing figures continue to increase,' she said, 'and the interest in me as a personality grows, I expect he'll stick to it, but there's no telling with these people.'

'What do you mean?

'Well . . . if I get invited to be a guest on, say, *Woman's Hour* or *Desert Island Discs*, or a quiz programme, it would be a big plug for the show and they would value it highly.'

'That's not likely, is it?' he said.

'Don't know. But it'll have to happen soon before the audience is fed up of seeing me. I'm sure they'll drop me like a red-hot brick if my appeal as an ordinary ex-dinner lady and part-time carer, who is a single parent and as poor as a church mouse no longer attracts big viewing figures.'

He laughed slightly. 'Oh, Mum, the audience is not going to get fed up with *you*. They all know of you at Cheapo's. They pull my leg about you. They think you're great. Most of them will be tuned in to see how you do on Sunday night.'

'That's nice, love, but Zenith Television count their viewers in *millions.* We must get these pots washed. Here!'

There was the sound of a moan from Tom Huxley.

Then she said, 'Come on. The quicker these are done, the sooner I can get to revising and the better chance I have to win you that yacht.'

'If you're still going to be given the answers,' he said, 'what's the point of revising?'

Crisp and Scrivens exchanged glances.

Josephine Huxley breathed in loud enough for it to travel through the ether to the eavesdroppers, and then in a loud voice said, *'In case he changes his mind.'* That was followed by a loud rattle of pots and cutlery.

Crisp took off his headphones. Scrivens took off his.

'Nearly but not quite,' Crisp said.

Scrivens nodded. 'I think the boss would want to know.'

'Yes. I'll ring him now.'

FIFTEEN

The following morning, at 8.28 a.m., as Angel was walking down the corridor to his office, he found himself singing.

Oh what a beautiful morning,
Oh what a beautiful day,
Everything's coming up roses,
Everything's going my way . . .

He quickly took off his coat and hat and put them on the hook glued to the stationery cupboard.

His phone rang.

He stopped singing, looked at it and snatched it up. 'Angel.'

It was Superintendent Harker. 'Dammit, why is your phone always busy when I want to speak to you?'

'Don't know, sir,' Angel said, not knowing what alternative reply he could have made.

'Come up here, right away,' Harker said.

Angel replaced the phone. His happy morning had suddenly taken a 180-degree turn.

He left his office and went up the corridor to Harker's office. He knocked on the door and pushed it open.

The powerful smell of menthol battered his nostrils like a hot blanket. The usual towers of boxes, papers, files, books, medications and thick brown envelopes covered the little man's desk.

'You wanted me, sir?' Angel said.

'Aye. Sit down. It's Friday, and I'm concerned about what you are planning to do about the two men you have out in Birmingham and the young lad you have in Leeds.'

'Valuable information is coming in from both locations, sir. Last night I heard from the Birmingham team. They now have a contestant's phone and her living room fitted with transmitters, and they have already heard and recorded firm information that somebody is supplying her with the answers to the questions.'

'Did they get the individual's name?'

'I'm afraid not, sir, but that's the basis of the motive, I believe, for both murders.'

'Maybe, but I'm sure you're aware that you can't use information recorded in such a way in court.'

'Of course,' Angel said. 'And the lad, Ahaz, undercover in the Leeds television studios, very nearly had the name.'

Harker sniffed then sighed. 'It's always "very nearly" but "not quite" with you, Angel, isn't it? It's never "positively". Well, I can't afford to pay for the gargantuan appetites of those men of yours out there, staying in five-star hotels over the weekend, as well as their overtime.'

The speed of Angel's breathing increased. He might have expected this sort of attitude from Harker. It was always the cost of the CID department that bothered him most of all.

'They're actually booked into a *three*-star hotel, sir,' Angel said.

'No matter. The cost of these sorts of jaunts is always astronomical.'

Angel suddenly felt a hot lump in his belly. It rose rapidly, mushroomed across his chest and spread up to his face, turning it scarlet.

'We have to have awareness about what expenses the taxpayer will see as reasonable and acceptable for this sort of inquiry,' Harker said.

Angel's fists were clenched. 'The taxpayer is *always* delighted when we manage to get the guilty convicted and put away for an appropriate term.'

'But you don't seem to be getting there, lad, do you?'

'I *am* getting there, sir. But if you take away the channels through which I acquire the necessary intelligence I won't be getting *anywhere*, will I?'

Harker shook his head. 'You always make this so personal,' he said.

'*You* make it personal. Whenever I am making progress in a case, you come along with some reason — usually the cost — as to why that course should be abandoned, and then you leave me stranded without that primary line of inquiry to pursue. And I have to start afresh.'

'You have to learn that this station is not here merely to provide *you* with employment and glorify your little successes to the media. The police service has many arms. Solving crime is only one of them, and I cannot allow it to be supported at the expense of any other. Because it's Friday, it is necessary to recall Crisp and Scrivens now, so that they can be in Bromersley by five o'clock and will therefore not be eligible for overtime or away from home expenses. All right?'

Angel had no choice. The superintendent had the rank and the authority.

'Right,' Angel said. 'What about Ahmed Ahaz in Leeds?'

'So far as the rest of this week is concerned, he must not remain in a situation of working beyond his regular hours nor should he be in left in a position where he can justifiably claim expenses.'

'And if he continues to deliver useful intelligence, can he continue where he is next week?'

Harker shuffled uneasily. He looked like a bus driver sat on a boil. 'I suppose so,' he said. 'But he had better not be filing any claim for expenses.'

Angel came out of the superintendent's office with his stomach in knots and his mind full of anger. He stormed his way down to his office: if anything had been in his way he would not have seen it. He sat in the swivel chair and tried to reduce the pile of paper but his concentration was shot. His mind was on the face of Trevor Crisp, who he was very shortly going to have to tell to pack up and come home even though — Angel was convinced — the team were on the very brink of overhearing the source of the answers to the quiz questions which would give them the identity of the murderer.

It was at that moment that Angel's mobile rang. It was Ahmed.

'Yes, lad? What's up?' Angel said.

'Good morning, sir,' Ahmed said. 'Well, it's a funny thing, sir. I didn't know what to do. This morning, I was summoned to the HR office, and when I got there it was to give me a wage. Well, I took it and signed for it. It would have looked fishy if I had declined it.'

'Aye. That's all right, lad. You did right. Put it in your pocket and hand it to the accounts office here when you're next in the station. And by the way, is it possible for you to get two tickets for Sunday evening's transmission of the show?'

'I should think so, sir. I'll ask my boss, manager of the post room. He'll know how to swing it.'

'If not, ask Berezin. He'll certainly be able to fix it.'

'Right, sir.'

'Good. And what time do you finish there today?'

'Friday is a four o'clock finish, sir. And the post distribution office doesn't open on Saturdays and Sundays.'

'And what time do you start on Monday morning?'

'Same as there, sir. 8.30,' Ahmed said. 'Am I working here for another week, sir?' he said, his eyes popping out.

Angel sensed he was pleased. 'You are. Hopefully to get some further information that will help me to close this case.'

'I know, sir. I'll do what I can. Goodbye, sir.'

Angel closed the mobile and pushed it back into his pocket.

Then, on his landline, he phoned Crisp and ordered him to close down the obbo and come home.

'You've served your purpose, Trevor,' Angel said. 'You've confirmed the motive that somebody at Zenith was giving the answers to the questions to the contestant, enabling her to win lots of money.'

'But we were very nearly given the name, sir,' Crisp said. 'It would have slipped out during the next few days, and certainly when she was celebrating or cursing on Monday morning.'

'I know all that. And I know that there have been two murders brought about by the villain needing the secret to be maintained. But we have Ahmed in the TV station. I'm expecting him to come out with the info soon. So let's have no more argument, Trevor, pack up and come home.'

He ended the call and banged down the phone. He hated curbing Crisp's enthusiasm. He was almost at the end of his tether with Harker. It would be a relief to get away from him for the weekend.

He reached into his pocket for his notes. He pulled out the brown envelope with the tiny writing on it and began to draw lines through the items he had dealt with. There was a knock at the door.

'Come in,' he called without looking up.

It was Leisha Baverstock. '*There* you are, sir. Couldn't find you anywhere. There's been a man on the phone going crazy because he couldn't reach you.'

Angel looked up. He was concerned. 'Did he leave a name?'

'Yes, sir. His name was Archie Ackroyd, of the estate agents, Ackroyd and Whitehouse. Do you know him?'

Angel's face muscles tightened. He snatched up the phone, looked up the number and clicked on it.

It was soon answered. It was Archie Ackroyd.

'It's Michael Angel. You been ringing me?'

Ackroyd sighed with relief. 'Ah, Michael, you asked me to let you know about anybody who inquired about The Brambles,' he said. 'Well, I've got a man here now. He wants to buy it. He says he doesn't need to see it. He isn't haggling either. He'll pay the asking price. He wants me to take his banker's draft for £25,000 as a deposit, and take it off the market. What do you want me to say to him?'

Five minutes later, Angel turned the BMW into Market Square in the centre of the business offices in Bromersley and parked on a yellow line. He put his 'Police on Duty' card on the dashboard then rushed through the door into the reception area of Ackroyd and Whitehouse's office. A girl behind the desk looked up. She looked worried.

'I'm Inspector Angel. Mr Ackroyd is expecting me.'

Her face flushed up. It was as red as the guilty light of a breathalyser. She pointed to a door. 'Through there, sir,' she said.

Angel went straight through and saw Ackroyd at his desk with a man seated opposite reading a document.

Ackroyd stood up and pointed at the man.

Angel recognized him. It was Dennis Grant. He had last seen him at Zenith Television, when he had interviewed him about Jeni Lowe.

Grant looked up. He recognized Angel. He looked across angrily at Ackroyd. 'Here,' he said. 'What is this?'

Angel said, 'I hear you are interested in buying The Brambles?'

Grant shrugged. 'I might have been. What's it got to do with the police?'

'Normally nothing but when you've been trying to scare a woman rigid so that you could pick up the house cheaply, it is everything to do with the police.'

'I don't know what you're talking about.'

'I think you do.'

'Look, I came here to buy a house. That's all I know. And I'm prepared to pay its advertised price. What's wrong with that?'

'The advertised price is wrong. I think you know that. Considering there's a fireplace in there that's made of gold.'

Grant's eyes glowed. 'That gold is *mine*,' he said. 'And I can prove it. It was put there by my father. Painted over for security reasons. It was his life's savings. My father told *me* about it years ago. It was for *me*, *not* for my sister. She's totally round the twist. Gone oriental. Having it off with old Charlie. *She* sold the house. Never even told me Dad was dead. It should never have been sold. My sister had no right to do that.'

Angel said, 'I don't think your wife knows you're thinking of buying The Brambles.'

'It's nothing to do with her.' He blinked in surprise and then looked back at Angel. 'How do you know my wife?'

Angel had made a stab in the dark. He hadn't known if Grant was married or not. 'Oh?' he continued. 'Are you buying it as a little love nest on the side for you and Cora then?'

Grant flinched at the mention of the girl's name. 'Who is this Cora you are referring to?'

'You know, you really *are* good,' Angel said. 'Your appearances as the villain, Amos Cudlipp, in the coat and stovepipe hat and then the disappearance of a silk skirt into the wardrobe were absolutely brilliant. And that trick of Cora not being to light a fire in the study and making sure nobody else could either . . . You nearly sent Mrs Helen Rose completely out of her mind. Do you realize that?'

'I don't know what you are talking about.'

'And do you know something interesting? Having worn that coat and that hat at least once means that something of you will be on the garments: a hair, a miniscule speck of dead skin less than the size of the smallest fragment of talcum powder, or some saliva or body odour. From that our forensic department will be able to determine the presence of your DNA, which will prove your guilt.'

'Absolute rubbish. I wasn't there. It wasn't me.'

'And what we can't corroborate by forensic science, we can rely on Cora to fill in the missing bits of evidence to put before a judge.'

'Huh! You can't rely on anything Cora says,' he said. He looked at Angel's determined face and said, 'I need a brief, a solicitor.'

'You certainly do,' Angel said.

There was a knock on the door and two burly police patrolmen came into the room.

Angel nodded towards them. 'Right on cue, lads.'

They advanced towards Grant, one of them unhooking a pair of handcuffs from his belt.

Angel said, 'Dennis Grant, I am arresting you on suspicion that you attempted to obtain property by deception. You do not have to say anything but . . .'

Angel returned to his office and immediately phoned the station desk sergeant. It was an old friend, DS Clifton.

'Ah, Bernie,' Angel said. 'Two patrolmen are bringing in a man called Dennis Grant for attempting to obtain property by deception. Find him a solicitor, will you? And allow him a phone call. And will you also send a couple of PCs to The Brambles, Havercroft Lane, off Sheffield Road to pick up a Cora Angelina Blenkinsop for questioning?'

'Right, sir.'

Angel replaced the phone. He sighed. He rubbed a hand hard against his chin. He was tired but the day had only just begun. He pulled the pile on his desk towards him and began to finger through some of the paperwork at the top.

Fifty minutes later, he had really made a difference to the pile. Then there was a knock at the door.

'Come in,' he called. It was patrolman PC Sean Donohue.

'I've put Cora Angelina Blenkinsop in interview room number one, sir. I assume that's all right?'

'Anybody with her?'

'Yes, sir. Leisha Baverstock.'

'Yes. Right. Thank you, Sean.'

The patrolman went out.

Angel closed the file he was reading, placed it on top of the pile and pushed it away. He made his way to the interview room two doors away.

Cora Blenkinsop was sitting opposite PC Leisha Baverstock, drinking tea out of a paper cup from the machine in the corridor.

Leisha stood up. Cora gawped at him.

'Right, thank you, Leisha.'

Leisha smiled and went out.

He sat down opposite Cora.

'What you brought me here for?' she said. 'Disgusting, two coppers knocking on my employer's address wanting to bring me in for questioning, as if I was a common criminal.'

'Now, Cora,' he said, 'this is a preliminary interview for me to decide whether or not to prosecute you for attempting to obtain property by deception. I am not recording this and there are no witnesses. If I do decide to prosecute, you will need a solicitor. Do you understand that?'

'I haven't done anything,' Cora Blenkinsop said. 'I mean, Dennis said that it wasn't really wrong because he said the house was his. His father left it to him, and his sister had stolen it. She hadn't told him his father was dead. He'd been dead three months and the house sold before Dennis knew anything about it. And he adored his father and his father adored him.'

'But Cora, if Dennis adored his father, he would have lived with him, or close by him, or visited him frequently, or spoken to him on the phone, wouldn't he? Every day or every week, surely? You said Hubert Grant had been dead three months before Dennis found out. If Dennis had thought anything about his father he would have known, wouldn't he? There's something wrong there. Where was he at that time?'

'He was living in Wakefield with his wife and kids. Lived there twelve years. And working at Zenith. I never thought.'

'And what was he going to do with the house when he got possession of it?'

'It was for us to live in. He was going to leave his wife and we were going to live there, and start all over again.'

'And what did he plan to do with all that gold?'

Cora looked at Angel and frowned. 'All what gold?'

Angel's eyebrows shot up. 'Didn't he tell you about the gold?'

She shook her head and sneered at him. 'No. What are you talking about?'

'Didn't he tell you not to let the Roses light a real fire in the study? Didn't you always have to make sure that the sticks and paper were always too damp to burn?'

'Well, yes. That's because he said that his father had deliberately had the chimney blocked off by stuffing something up it to keep the room warm, and that it would billow out black smoke if a real fire was lit.'

'Well, why didn't you tell Mrs Rose that?'

'Because Dennis said not to. He said it would make for another bit of fun and spookiness.'

'That's what he told you?'

The muscles round her mouth tightened. 'I've *told* you,' she said.

Angel rubbed his chin.

Then Cora said, 'Now, what's all this about gold?'

SIXTEEN

The manager and Ahmed were very busy in the post room of Zenith Studios, Leeds: the manager was snuggled in a corner with a newspaper folded small and a pencil, trying to pick out a winner in the four o'clock at Kempton Park while Ahmed was sorting the three sacks of mail just delivered by the post office.

The phone rang. The manager was next to it. He pulled a face and reached out for the handset. 'Post room manager.'

It was the unmistakable voice of Viktor Berezin. 'I vant you to collect a small parcel which contains a videotape for urgent despatch to Japan. It will require a customs declaration certificate. Will you send somebody up for it?'

'Right away, Mr Berezin,' he said. He replaced the phone and turned to Ahmed and said, 'That's that Russian fella. Thinks he owns the place. Go up there and collect a parcel. For urgent despatch, *he* says, *on a Friday*, huh! That's what he thinks. Room 507. Fifth floor.'

'All right. I know the way,' Ahmed said.

He caught the lift to the fifth floor, got out when it stopped and made his way left along a corridor to the seventh door, which was on the corner of the building and the largest office on that floor.

He tapped on the door and went in.

Berezin was standing behind his desk looking at a pasty-faced young woman with long blonde hair on the other side holding a notebook and pencil. There was a small packet on the desk in front of him.

'It needs a customs declaration label,' Berezin said. 'Haven't we got one?'

'I'll have to check,' the young blonde woman said. She walked slowly out of the office, like a leopard. Ahmed watched her go.

Berezin looked at Ahmed. 'Won't be a minute, young man. We need a customs declaration label. Have you any in the post room?'

'I'm sorry. I don't really know. I haven't seen one. I have no idea what they look like.'

Berezin rubbed his chin. 'Hmm. I show you. I had a package of a videotape sent from New York this morning. The wrapping's probably in ze rubbish.'

He bent down, picked up the wastepaper basket and put it on his desk. 'I shouldn't have to be doing all zis,' Berezin grumbled.

There wasn't much in the basket but as Berezin fished around in what there was, Ahmed saw a small blue plastic top or cap identical to the one he remembered Angel had been trying to identify. The one left by the murderer under the seat in Jeni Lowe's car.

Berezin pulled a face. 'Nossing here,' he said. He grabbed the basket and sulkily banged it down at the side of his desk.

The young woman slinked back into the room. She was all hair, all smiles and waving something at the Russian. 'We've a whole new pad of them,' she said.

Ahmed took the opportunity and dived into the wastepaper basket to retrieve the plastic gizmo. He slipped it into his pocket. Nobody seemed to notice.

Berezin smiled at the woman. Ahmed had not seen him smile before. It was not a convincing sight.

'Give it to ze postman,' Berezin said.

She passed the pad of customs declaration labels across the desk to Ahmed.

'Thank you,' Ahmed said and made for the door.

Berezin called out. 'Hey! Postie!'

Ahmed felt his face go red. He stopped and turned.

'Haven't you forgotten somesing?' Berezin said with another big smile.

Ahmed frowned. His mouth dropped open. He couldn't think what he might have forgotten, unless it was something to do with the blue plastic thing he had taken.

Berezin pointed to the packet to be posted still on his desk. 'You've forgotten zis.'

Ahmed relaxed his breathing and returned to the desk. 'Sorry, sir,' he said, then he picked up the packet and went out.

'Strange young man,' the woman said, running a hand through her long blonde hair.

Ahmed went out of the office bursting with excitement. He was pleased to have the empty lift to himself. As it travelled to the ground floor, he examined the blue gizmo for any giveaway clue as to the owner or what use it could possibly have had. He discovered neither but he knew he must urgently tell Angel about his find.

Zenith Studio Two, Leeds, Yorkshire
Sunday, 24 November 2013, 9.30 p.m.

Angel and his wife had just seen an episode of *Wanna Be Rich?* broadcast live from Zenith Studios in Leeds. Thanks to Ahmed, they had been on the front row of the studio audience. Their hands were sore with all the clapping.

They had seen Josephine Huxley answer correctly the twelve questions put to her by the charming Alan de Souza, and she had won a further sum of £42,000.

They had been encouraged by a man in a red suit to clap and applaud vigorously at every twist and turn of the show.

The show had ended and Angel had turned to Mary and said, 'I want to go backstage, would you like to come with me?'

Her bright eyes got brighter. 'Oh yes,' she said.

'Come on then,' he said.

By the time they had found the right door and been allowed access by studio security, the contestants and Alan de Souza were leaving. There were a few members of the crew standing by.

As always, de Souza was met by Marie, his gofer with the trolley, who went through the routine of taking his microphone, battery, transmitter and earpiece receiver, and passing him in turn a glass of cool water, his inhaler and a towel.

'Congratulations, Mr de Souza,' Angel said. 'May I introduce my wife, Mary?'

Alan de Souza smiled as he patted his perspiring forehead with the towel. 'Very pleased to meet you, Mrs Angel. You should come out to dinner with me some evening,' he said. 'Preferably when your husband is out on his investigations,' he added, with a mischievous grin.

Mary laughed.

Angel smiled. 'It could never happen, Mr de Souza. I find it impossible to leave her, even for an evening. Her cooking is out of this world.'

'I thought by definition beautiful women couldn't cook.'

Angel smiled. 'Tonight,' he said, 'you have met the exception.'

De Souza smiled and said, 'I will let you have the last word, Inspector.' Then he turned to Mary and said, 'You will excuse me, my work is not quite done. There are some matters I *have* to attend to.'

'Of course,' she said. 'Nice to have met you, Mr de Souza.'

'And you also,' he said and rushed off.

A young man who Angel noticed had been hovering nearby took the opportunity of approaching him. 'Inspector Angel? You might not remember me. I'm the floor manager here, Jed Morrison.'

'Of course, I do, Mr Morrison,' Angel said. 'This is my wife.'

Morrison looked at Mary and nodded politely. She smiled back.

'Can I ask you . . . I understand that you've had our director, Dennis Grant, arrested for something. What exactly has he done?'

'Well, he's been arrested on suspicion of attempting to obtain property by deception. Why, what do you know about the case?'

'Oh, nothing,' Morrison said quickly. 'I don't know anything about *that*.'

Angel rubbed his chin. 'Do you know anything about the death of Jeni Lowe or Antony Edward Abercrombie, then?'

'No. No. You already asked me.'

Viktor Berezin appeared from nowhere and said, 'Excuse me, Inspector, if you please, but Jed is wanted urgently by our new director.'

Morrison looked up. 'Oh?' he said. He looked at Angel. 'Will you excuse me, Inspector?'

'Of course,' Angel said. 'Please carry on. We don't want to be a nuisance.' He looked at Mary and added, 'Do we, darling?'

'Of course not,' Mary said.

Jed Morrison dashed off.

Berezin turned and began to walk away.

Angel called after him. 'Mr Berezin.'

The Russian looked back. 'We have nothing to say to each other, I think, Inspector Angel,' he said. 'You get me to arrange a job for your young policeman in ze post office here, then you repay me by arresting my director and had him locked up. That meant that I had to replace him at very short notice. I have been frantic vis worry that he could direct the show to standard. But vis my help we have managed it, I think. But *please* do not arrest anybody else from my show. Good night to you.'

He turned and walked off.

It was 8.28 a.m. the following morning, Monday, 25 November, when Angel arrived at his office in Bromersley police station.

His incursion into Zenith Studios the previous evening had not produced any further clues. As far as he could see, none of the suspects there had given themselves away and yet he was positive that the murderer of Jeni Lowe and Antony Edward Abercrombie was either Viktor Berezin or somebody else who worked at Zenith Studios. Furthermore, he believed that whoever it was, he or she was still making money out of Zenith Studios that benefited Josephine Huxley and possibly other smaller winning contestants as well as the crook himself.

The phone rang. He reached out for it.

It was Harker, coughing his head off. Eventually he said, 'Come up here, lad. Straightaway.'

Angel replaced the phone, pulled a face and got up from the desk. He arrived outside Superintendent Harker's office, knocked on the door and let himself in. As he expected, the office smelled like a chemist's shop in a heatwave.

The superintendent was still coughing and the recurrent tiring effort had caused bright pink patches to appear on his cheeks.

He pointed a finger downwards to indicate to Angel to sit down.

At length he stopped coughing, disposed of the tissue he was holding, and looked across the desk.

'Now then, Angel, have they got back safely?'

'Who, sir?'

'Crisp and Scrivens, lad. They have been on an obbo in Birmingham, haven't they?'

'Oh. I assume so, sir. On your instructions, I ordered them back. I'm sure they will have returned.'

'I thought you would have known.'

'It's only just gone 8.30, sir.'

'Do you see your job as an office-hours-only job then? Do you not see — in your role as a senior officer — that your responsibilities do not necessarily end at five o'clock on a Friday and begin again at 8.30 on Monday morning?'

'I am frequently working out of hours, sir. In fact I was working last night until after ten o'clock at Zenith Studios, Leeds.'

Harker sniffed then said, 'Did you manage to get yourself in front of the cameras then?'

Angel's lips tightened back against his teeth. 'No, sir,' he said. 'It became necessary, as you had taken away my opportunity of listening in on Josephine Huxley, the top winner of the show *Wanna Be Rich*?, who would of course by now *almost certainly* — having won an additional £42,000 — have mentioned the name of the one giving her all the answers.'

'That is pure conjecture.'

'The odds are that she or her son would have let it slip. I already have the son on tape confirming that his mother *was* being given the answers. Why not the name tripping off his or her tongue speaking casually about the person who supplied them?'

'It is still only conjecture.'

Angel was fuming. 'Everything that hasn't yet happened in this life, sir, is conjecture. It stops becoming conjecture when it has become fact. I am talking about the possibility, the probability, the also damned bloody likelihood of what might have happened!'

Harker stared at him, his purple lips quivering. 'Are you swearing at me, lad?'

'Not *at* you, sir. No. I use the word for emphasis.'

There was a moment or two of silence.

Harker's chest heaved. He was having some difficulty breathing. His face was scarlet. His shoulders were hunched and lowered in quick succession. His breathing was laboured.

Angel wondered if he needed medical attention.

Harker reached over the desk for something. His fingers fumbled around, searching. He found it. It was a small, medicated vapour spray. He pulled off the mouthpiece cover and dropped it on the desk.

The mouthpiece cover caught Angel's eye.

Harker put the inhaler opening to his mouth and pressed the bottom of the canister several times. The aerosol sprayed medicated vapour into his mouth. It travelled along his air passages to his lungs.

In a few seconds, his breathing became slower. He closed his eyes briefly as he enjoyed the relief. His face was returning to normal, the colour of the lavatory walls at Pentonville.

Angel reached across the desk and picked up the mouthpiece of the inhaler. He looked at it. Then he reached down into his pocket and took out the one found in Jeni Lowe's car. He put them together. They were identical.

His heart leaped and then began to thump as if it was trying to get out of his chest. He remembered the one person on his shortlist of suspects who also used a vapour spray. That person was the murderer of Jeni Lowe and Antony Edward Abercrombie. It was Alan de Souza.

He looked across at Harker, who was looking round his desk for something.

Angel still had the two mouthpiece covers in his hand. He held one up. 'Looking for this, sir?'

Harker snatched it off him and in a strained voice said, 'Get on with it then. And remember what I said.'

Angel's mind was very busy. There was a lot to do. He couldn't help but think that that was the first time Harker had ever assisted him in solving a case.

As he arrived at his office, Crisp and Scrivens were waiting for him.

'Come in,' he said. 'Got an urgent job for you two. First get a warrant to arrest Alan de Souza for the murder of Jeni Lowe and Antony Edward Abercrombie. Then go to Zenith Television and arrest him.'

The phone rang. Angel reached out for it.

It was Don Taylor. 'I've had an email this morning from the lab in Wetherby reporting that the DNA of the hair and hair follicles on the black coat, stovepipe hat and the silk skirt found in the cavity at the back of the Roses' wardrobe match that of Dennis Grant.'

Angel smiled. 'Thank you, Don. That makes that case cast iron. I will advise the CPS.'

'I thought you'd like to know, sir.'

Angel replaced the phone.

It was an hour later, at 10.30 a.m., when the phone rang again. Angel reached out for it. It was Crisp ringing from Leeds. 'De Souza is not here, sir. He hasn't turned out for work. There's always a meeting of the key people of the show at ten o'clock the morning after transmission. Well, he's not shown up for it, which is very unusual.'

Angel didn't like the sound of that. 'Who have you been speaking to?'

'Mr Berezin's secretary, sir.'

Angel frowned. 'I didn't know he had one. What's her name and what does she look like?'

'Didn't catch her name, sir, but she has long blonde hair and a pasty face.'

'Don't know her,' Angel said. 'Well, find out de Souza's home address and follow it through, quick as you can. Also ask them if there is any club or place where he might have sought shelter or accommodation. Girlfriend or relation. We *must* find him.'

'Right, sir.'

Angel tapped in Ahmed's mobile number. It rang a long time before he answered. 'Is it all right to talk, Ahmed?'

'I'm in the lift on my own. I'm OK for a minute, sir.'

'Well, quickly, I have sent DS Crisp and DC Scrivens to arrest Alan de Souza but they can't find him. Have you any idea where he might be?'

'No, sir. Is he the murderer?'

'Yes, lad. I believe it's cut and dried but we've got to find him. So I want you back here ASAP. Make it all right with the people in Human Resources and come home.'

'Right, sir.'

Angel replaced the phone and rubbed his chin. Perhaps de Souza, anticipating his arrest, had run off somewhere. Perhaps he was at home, ill? Perhaps the moon was made of Strangeways' Yorkshire pudding. It was no good, he would have to be patient. There was a lot of desk work to be done, so he reached out to the pile.

About an hour later, Angel's phone rang again.

It was Crisp. 'De Souza's not at home, sir. We broke into his flat on the outskirts and it looks as if he might have packed a bag and left in a hurry. We've asked the neighbours. They know him but they've no idea of his likely whereabouts.'

Angel sighed. That's about the worst that could have happened. A rich young man not burdened with familial ties could so easily disappear to some other part of the world and start up a new life if he wanted.

'Where are you now?'

'Inside his flat, sir.'

'Any photographs of him anywhere around? Is his passport there? Have a look. Set Scrivens on it. I'll hold on.'

Two minutes later, Crisp said, 'No, sir. We can't find any photographs at all. And his passport isn't here.'

Angel blew out a yard of air. It didn't look good. 'Right. Go back to Zenith TV and see Berezin. Or that blonde with the pasty face and the long hair. Ask them for a recent photograph of de Souza, the sort of thing we can copy and give out to the newspapers and television news.'

'You going to make a national appeal, sir?'

'If you don't find him, Trevor, there's no alternative. He's a murderer on the loose.'

SEVENTEEN

After a hectic Monday morning, Angel had an equally hectic afternoon. He notified the press and the television people that Alan de Souza was wanted for murder, he furnished them with a recent photograph and he requested them to ask the public for help in finding him. The sound and television media had already run the story from six o'clock that evening, and the national daily papers were running it in their first editions this coming morning.

He also notified all the airports, seaports and UK border guards.

Having done all that he could do, Angel went home to the beautiful Mary, had a meal, watched an hour of TV, and was now in bed sleeping the sleep of the good.

That late November night, the sky was bright, the stars were sparkling, and Jack Frost was casting his cold spell over the paths, roads and roofs of the land.

In the distance, a church clock chimed three. Angel opened his eyes. He was wide awake. He turned his head to the left to check the clock on his bedside cabinet. The luminous paint on the hands indicated that it was either a quarter past twelve or three o'clock. He was inclined to agree with the church clock. He then looked to his right. He couldn't see Mary, but he could hear her gentle even breathing. She sounded fine.

Then he heard a noise he couldn't explain. It sounded like a pan being knocked off the pan stand in the kitchen. It was easily done. You only had to brush by and catch a pan handle that might be sticking out a little way and down the pan went, landing on the tiled kitchen floor, making a fair old rattle.

Keeping very still, he listened. A few seconds later, he heard another noise. His heart began to thump. Somebody *was* downstairs. He regularized his breathing and whisked back the duvet. He pushed his feet into his slippers and made his way silently out of the bedroom, along the landing and down the stairs. As he reached the bottom step, he saw flickers of light and shadows from a small torch in the sitting room. He silently approached the door and saw a figure with long blonde hair and a pasty complexion. The figure had pulled open the sideboard drawer and was looking inside it. Angel swiftly made his way into the room behind the settee across to the library table and switched on the reading lamp. The intruder turned back from the sideboard and gasped.

Angel blinked. He did not recognize the intruder.

'Who are you and what do you want?' Angel said.

The intruder stared at him and said nothing.

'What do you want?' Angel said.

The intruder pulled out a gun and pointed it at him. Angel recognized it as a Walther PPX. An old model, but it would kill anybody at that range.

'Put up your hands,' the intruder said.

As he raised his hands, Angel changed the angle of his right hand and knocked the reading lamp on the library table over. The light went out. The room was in darkness.

Angel dived to the floor.

The intruder fired off three shots in the direction of where Angel had been.

Angel crawled round the back of the settee to the sideboard, stood up, grabbed a heavy green glass door stop that had stood many years at his grandmother's back door, leaned over the settee and banged it across the back of the intruder's head.

The firing stopped. The intruder went down with a crash.

Angel rushed to the doorway and switched on the central light.

He saw the Walther PPX on the carpet and kicked it out of the way. He looked at the long blonde flowing hair and reached down to touch the face. It wasn't flesh he could feel but rubber. He realized it was a rubber face mask. He peeled it off under the chin and over the back of the head to reveal Alan de Souza.

Mary, in her nightdress, came running in. She put her arms round him. 'Are you all right, darling? Whatever's happening?'

'It's all right, Mary. Everything's all right.'

Two hours later, peace descended on the Angel household. Alan de Souza had been charged by the night duty sergeant and taken away. The Walther PPK had been put in an evidence bag and taken to the station safe, and Grandmother's door stop, undamaged, had been replaced on the sideboard.

Michael and Mary Angel were still in their night clothes but neither party was tired enough to go back to bed.

They were having a very early breakfast.

Mary passed a cup of tea and said, 'What I don't understand is what de Souza was up to?'

Angel reached out for a piece of toast and said, 'Well, with some big winners, de Souza arranged to give the contestant the answers to the questions for a hefty proportion of that contestant's winnings. The contestants weren't ever likely to report the fiddle to anybody, were they? He had a sure-fire easy way of making money, in theory forever. He had his own private money tree.'

'Well, what went wrong?'

'His new girlfriend, Jeni Lowe, found out about it and told him that he should stop it or she'd spill the beans. He had no intention of stopping and so he killed her by fixing the brakes of her car. But she didn't die before she told old

Abercrombie — who was out scavenging for fuel for his fire — the facts and asked him to tell the police. But he didn't do that. Instead he tried to blackmail de Souza. And was also murdered by him.'

'How awful. But are you going to be able to prove that de Souza's the murderer?'

'Oh yes. There was the mouthpiece cover from an inhaler the same as he uses, plus fingerprints all over the interior of Jeni Lowe's car, and there were a few hairs on Abercrombie's chest and on his hand. If those prints and those hairs are de Souza's, and I fully expect that they will be, it will prove his guilt; also it will show what a liar he is. De Souza had said that he'd *never* been out with Jeni Lowe, *never* been in her car and had *never* heard of old man Abercrombie.'

Angel slowly went upstairs to shower, shave and dress, then got down to the station for his usual time of 8.28 a.m. As he made his way down the corridor, everybody was smiling and without exception spoke to him, if it was only to say, 'Good morning.'

He arrived at his office and closed the door. He took off his coat and hat and sat down at his desk. He smiled. He was thinking it was great being a copper as long as you solve your cases. If you can't, you might just as well be a traffic policeman.

He looked at the pile of paperwork in front of him. He wrinkled his nose then reached out and dragged it forward.

There was a knock at the door. 'Come in,' he said.

It was DS Flora Carter holding a sheet of A4. 'Good morning, sir, and congratulations.'

He smiled again. 'Thank you, Flora. But you did your bit, as did everybody else. Did you get my message?'

'Yes, sir,' Flora said, waving the sheet of A4. 'I have it here. A copy of de Souza's bank statement, sir, and he has a credit balance of over £680,000.'

Angel's eyebrows shot up.

Quoting from the bank statement, Flora said, 'It is made up from cash amounts paid in almost every Monday morning over the past three months, after the transmission of the show on a Sunday night. For instance the last three Monday mornings, he paid in £6,000, £31,000, and £75,000 respectively. Those figures are fifty per cent of the amount the winner Josephine Huxley won.'

'Wow!' Angel said. 'Great stuff, Flora. Leave that statement with me. The CPS will be delighted to have it. Cherry on the cake. Thank you.'

She went out.

There was another knock on the door. 'Come in,' he called.

It was Ahmed. The wrinkles on his brow indicated that he was in some distress.

'What's the matter, lad?' asked Angel.

'Oh, sir, I have just seen that neighbour of mine . . . the one that I got this Mitto-Amino watch from,' he said, holding up his wrist. 'He's in the charge room with the duty sergeant. He's being booked for selling counterfeit goods!'

THE END

ALSO BY ROGER SILVERWOOD

YORKSHIRE MURDER MYSTERIES

Book 1: THE MISSING NURSE
Book 2: THE MISSING WIFE
Book 3: THE MAN IN THE PINK SUIT
Book 4: THE MORALS OF A MURDERER
Book 5: THE AUCTION MURDERS
Book 6: THE MISSING KILLER
Book 7: THE UMBRELLA MURDERS
Book 8: THE MISSING MILLIONAIRE
Book 9: THE MISSING THIEF
Book 10: FIND THE LADY
Book 11: THE MISSING MODEL
Book 12: MURDER IN BARE FEET
Book 13: THE MISSING HUSBAND
Book 14: THE CUCKOO CLOCK MURDERS
Book 15: SHRINE TO MURDER
Book 16: THE SNUFFBOX MURDERS
Book 17: THE DOG COLLAR MURDERS
Book 18: THE CHESHIRE CAT MURDERS
Book 19: THE DIAMOND ROSARY MURDERS
Book 20: THIRTEEN STEPS TO MURDER
Book 21: THE FRUIT GUM MURDERS
Book 22: THE MONEY TREE MURDERS

FREE KINDLE BOOKS AND OFFERS

Do you love mysteries, historical fiction and romance? Join 1,000s of readers enjoying great books through our mailing list. You'll get new releases and great deals every week from one of the UK's leading independent publishers.

Join today, and you'll get your first bargain book this month!

www.joffebooks.com

Follow us on Facebook, Twitter and Instagram @joffebooks

Thank you for reading this book. If you enjoyed it please leave feedback on Amazon or Goodreads, and if there is anything we missed or you have a question about, then please get in touch. The author and publishing team appreciate your feedback and time reading this book.

We're very grateful to eagle-eyed readers who take the time to contact us. Please send any errors you find to corrections@joffebooks.com. We'll get them fixed ASAP.

Printed in Great Britain
by Amazon

58360451R00106